"Didn't mea

"Well, you did," .... whole thing scared me. A vigilante hanging in 1995—who would have thought it possible?"

Ryder started. "You *are* shook up. You mean 1885."

"No, of course I don't!" she snapped, her hands flattened against his chest and pushed. "Though considering what happened today, it *should* be 1885."

Her lovely mouth gaped open, and Ryder was hard-pressed not to act on the instinct to taste it. He stepped back and took a better look at her apparel—pants, shirt, vest, leather boots. "Uh, you do know you're a woman, right?"

"I beg your pardon?"

"Well, you *are* dressed in men's clothing."

Gaze narrowing, she asked, "What century are you living in, bub?"

Ryder felt the short hairs at the back of his neck rise, and a chill shot down his spine. Something weird was going on here. Something out of his experience.

Dear Reader,

What else can be more romantic *and* more mysterious than traveling through time to meet the man who was destined to share your life? We're especially proud to present TIMELESS LOVE, a unique program in Harlequin Intrigue that showcases these much-loved time-travel stories.

As a girl, Patricia Rosemoor wanted to be Annie Oakley—probably the reason she was determined to learn to ride even if she did live in the heart of Chicago, a city without a single stable. In her first time-travel Intrigue, Patricia finally had her chance to be a sharpshooting, hard-riding woman of the Old West, fulfilling that childhood fantasy at last.

We hope you enjoy *The Desperado*...and all the special books coming to you in the months ahead in TIMELESS LOVE.

Sincerely,

Debra Matteucci
Senior Editor and Editorial Coodinator
Harlequin Books
300 East 42nd Street, Sixth Floor
New York, New York 10017

The

Desperado

Patricia Rosemoor

Harlequin Books

TORONTO • NEW YORK • LONDON
AMSTERDAM • PARIS • SYDNEY • HAMBURG
STOCKHOLM • ATHENS • TOKYO • MILAN
MADRID • WARSAW • BUDAPEST • AUCKLAND

To Cheryl and Rick,
for intriguing me into seeing Santa Fe firsthand

ISBN 0-373-22346-3

THE DESPERADO

Copyright © 1995 Patricia Pinianski

This edition published by arrangement with Harlequin Books S.A.

Printed in U.S.A.

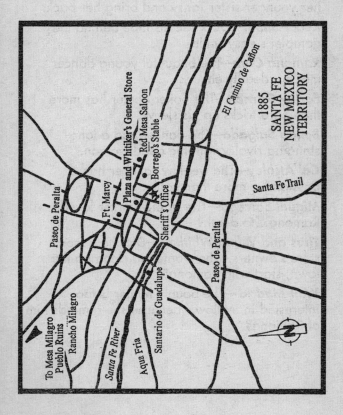

1885
SANTA FE
NEW MEXICO
TERRITORY

El Camino de Cañon

Santa Fe Trail

Paseo de Peralta

Paseo de Peralta

Plaza and Whitiker's General Store

Red Mesa Saloon

Borrego's Stable

Ft. Marcy

Sheriff's Office

To Mesa Milagro
Pueblo Ruins

Rancho Milagro

Santa Fe River

Aqua Fria

Santario de Guadalupe

CAST OF CHARACTERS

Willow Kane—She would do anything to find her younger sister Tansy and bring her back.

Ryder Smith—Dark secrets hide behind the gambler's easy smile.

Ramona Cruz—The beautiful young dancer made a deadly enemy.

Farley Garnett—The poker dealer has more than card tricks up his sleeve.

Benita Salgado—The dancer had a long-standing rivalry with the dead woman.

Cal Atchley—The wealthy rancher had a passion for more than cattle.

Miguel Borrego—The stable worker loved Ramona...to death?

Titus and Velma Whitiker—Did the general store's owners, who wanted to clean up the town, start with Ramona?

Wolf Madrid—The bounty hunter is too interested in Willow...because she reminds him of Ramona?

Prologue

New Mexico Territory, 1885

The sun hung low in the west, casting liquid fire over the New Mexican landscape. Ryder Smith took one last, long look around at the Wild West country he'd grown to feel part of—across a stretch of sandy earth to the east, Mesa Milagro quivering and dancing and burning a deep copper; in contrast, a sky of purest blue, the like of which he'd found nowhere else on earth; finally, the deep green of piñon and juniper, whose scent hung heavy on the air.

"A right fine day for a hanging!" yelled the leader of the vigilantes that had waylaid him. "String 'im up, boys!"

Ryder dug in his heels and tried to fight, but his hands were tied behind his back. Besides, including the leader, there were three of them, and even with his hands free and holding two Colt .45s, he wouldn't bet he'd survive. They were animals, predators—the scent of death already strong in their nostrils.

"Any of you boys got enough guts to show your faces?" Ryder demanded as he was lifted up onto the saddle of his horse and led under the shelter of a cottonwood.

All three wore bandannas to protect their worthless hides. Even so, he was certain he recognized Cal Atchley's cowpunchers—Buck, Atchley's foreman, and Caesar and Dexter—for all the good that would do him.

"Ain't no never mind who we be," Buck stated. "Just know we're here to see justice done."

"If I'm a murderer, why didn't Sheriff Landry arrest me when he had the chance?"

"'Cause he's a stupid fool."

The leader gestured to Caesar, who was already mounted. Caesar sidled in next to Ryder, looped rope in hand. But Ryder wasn't about to offer his neck for a noose. He waited all quietlike until the loop was lifted ... then gave his horse the signal to bolt. The gelding danced away from the other mount, but one of the masked men held the reins firm.

"What in tarnation are you fools doing?" Buck demanded, stepping forward to bully the animal back in place. "We don't got all day. Sun's about to set. Now get to it."

The rope whooshed toward Ryder's head. He ducked, but not fast enough. The loop landed square on his shoulders. And when he continued to struggle, the noose snugged around his neck.

"Any last words?" asked Caesar, who threw the other end of the rope up over a sturdy limb.

"I tell you I didn't kill her!"

But the faded blue eyes above the bandanna didn't blink as the hangman tightened the rope so Ryder had to stretch up in his stirrups. "Say your prayers, son."

Before Ryder could even think how to start, Buck yelled, "Hi-i-i-yah!" and slapped the rump of Ryder's mount.

At the same time, Dexter dropped the reins while dancing out of the way. No matter that Ryder held on to the saddle with all the might his legs could muster, he was ripped free in seconds. The weight of his body jerked downward. The noose tightened savagely, strangling him.

And, ready or not, unable to get so much as a swallow of air, pinpricks of bright light dancing before his eyes, Ryder went to meet his maker.

Chapter One

Willow Kane went in search of her younger sister with all the enthusiasm of a hound whose nap before a nice comfortable fire had been disturbed. Grandpa Jonah had offered to speak to Tansy for her, but she feared the old man would be too harsh on the teenager, who reminded him of his wayward daughter. Indeed, with her wild red hair and green eyes, Tansy was the spitting image of a younger Audrey Kane. And their grandpa feared that if Tansy wasn't held in check with a firm hand, she would take after their mama in every way.

He had a point.

Tansy always had been a wild child from the day Mama had brought them to live permanently with Grandpa Jonah. Tansy had been only three, Willow thirteen. Neither of them had ever understood why Mama had deserted them, and Grandpa had never seemed inclined to explain. But from that day on, Willow had learned the meaning of responsibility until she was sick to death of it.

First, she'd become a mother to her younger sister. Then, at eighteen, instead of going on to college after graduation like her classmates, she'd turned down a scholarship and had taken on more responsibility around the spread. Rancho Milagro had been going downhill because of the sour economy and Grandpa Jonah's stubbornness—he tended to dig in his heels rather than change with the times. But the ranch was her grandpa's life, and Willow owed him. Jonah Kane might be the owner and titular head of the spread, but Willow was the one who ran it now. She couldn't let the place die without a fight. Trouble was, she was just plain tired of fighting.

She found her sister down by the small corral watching the new mustangs rather than getting at her chores. Tansy was standing on a split rail, dressed in tight jeans and a fancy, embroidered Western shirt, her wild curly hair poking out from an ornate silver clasp studded with a turquoise stone the same green as her eyes—a birthday present from Willow, as was the matching bracelet Tansy also wore. She noted her sister's chestnut gelding Madrid was saddled, his reins looped around a nearby post.

As if sensing another presence, Tansy glanced over her shoulder, frowned, then jumped to the ground, advancing on Madrid as if she meant to ignore Willow.

"Tansy, we need to talk."

The fifteen-year-old stopped and rolled her eyes. "Talk? I know that tone. You mean you're going to give me another lecture."

Willow sighed. "I don't mean to lecture you—"

"Hell, if you don't."

"Tansy Kane, you watch your mouth!"

"Tansy, watch what you say," the teenager mimicked. "Tansy, watch how you act." She shook a warning finger as Grandpa would do to her, then, her demeanor changing to sullen, crossed her arms over her chest and took a step back. "Next you'll be telling me what to think."

Willow counted silently until she got her anger under control. She refused to lose her temper, exactly what Tansy would like her to do.

"I got a call from your school. Mrs. Sanchez said you told her you had a sick stomach, but that when she went to check on you, you hadn't reported to the nurse. She suspects you meant to cut your English class."

Tansy shifted guiltily, but protested, "I had a good reason."

"Which would be?"

Tansy stuck out a belligerent chin. "I had to get something, that's all."

Willow stood, arms crossed, booted foot tapping the dusty earth. "I'm waiting."

The siblings locked gazes in a silent duel. Willow knew she could wait out her passionate younger sister, no matter how long it took. Her mother had always said Willow had not only the exotic looks of her half-Indian father, but his bearing and patience, while Tansy had inherited the quick temper of *her* daddy. Mama had been right. As always, Tansy was the first to break the deadlock.

"Good grief, I just went to buy a book, okay!" the girl said, her green eyes flashing. "Is that an *appropriate* enough reason to skip an English class?"

Though relieved—for Tansy's exploits were, more often than not, more on the risky and adventurous side—Willow didn't relent. "So you bought a book for your class?"

"Not exactly."

"More Wolf Madrid, bounty hunter."

Ever since Tansy had found a box of dime novels in the ranch's original, now-deserted house, she'd had an obsession with the stories of the Wild West of yesteryear. Willow often thought Tansy got ideas for her more outrageous exploits straight out of the dusty yellow pages penned in the last century by an ancestor, T. S. Kane.

Like the time the year before when Tansy went on a survival outing into the high desert, equipped with nothing but her horse and a single canteen of water to seek out her adulthood the Indian way—the fictional Wolf Madrid was a half-breed and had offered the example. Thankfully, Tansy had let her intentions slip to one of the younger ranch hands. Still, they'd had to send a search party out after her and hadn't caught up to her until morning.

"Actually, this was a different one—*McCreery and the Quick-draw Kid,*" Tansy said excitedly, pulling the dusty tome from her back pocket and showing it to Willow. "I didn't even know old T.S. wrote anything but Wolf Madrid stories."

The faded gold cover portrayed a sketched gunfight in progress. The closer of the gunmen had fair hair and a dark mustache. The other was just a boy with long sideburns, longer dark hair, and a harelip marring his otherwise handsome face.

Willow sighed. "You're grounded for a week."

"What? For missing one measly class?"

"This isn't the first class. I hope it'll be the last. Since you'll have so much spare time, we'll ask Mrs. Sanchez for a project to keep you busy."

"That's unfair."

"Life's unfair."

"You're not my mother."

Tansy was fond of reminding her of that fact. Willow's temper flared. "Maybe you should go live with Mama . . . if she'd have you!"

She regretted the heated words even as they shot out of her mouth. Tansy's face paled, her freckles popping in contrast. They'd both been affected by their mother's desertion, but Tansy more than she. Audrey Kane lived in nearby Santa Fe, but she rarely saw them other than for a brief appearance at Rancho Milagro during the holidays or on the girls' birthdays. Mama always brought presents and pretty words but never offered so much as an invitation for her daughters to visit her in town.

"Tansy, I'm sorry—"

"No, you're not. I'm a trial to you. Miss Perfect Willow Kane, who's never done one thing wrong in her entire life. Well, I'm not you. I can't live up to Grandpa Jonah's standards!"

"No one expects you to be perfect—"

"He does. You do. Well, maybe I will go live with Mama!" Tansy shouted, stuffing the dime novel into her back pocket as she stalked over to Madrid.

"Tansy!"

But her sister ignored her.

Removing her hat where she'd slung it over the saddle horn, Tansy stuffed it onto her head, then mounted. "I'm getting out of here and never coming back!"

A statement that chilled Willow. She'd never known her own father—nor had Tansy known hers. They hardly had a relationship with their mother, and their grandpa was a hard man to get close to. All they really had was each other.

"Tansy, please don't say such a thing."

But her sister was already off, riding east toward Mesa Milagro. Knowing she had to let her go—that the angry teenager needed a way to let off steam—Willow headed for the house, cursing herself for the temper that had bested her long enough for her to hurt the one person in the world who meant everything to her.

She'd no sooner set one booted foot on the front stoop, when the screen door opened and Grandpa Jonah came outside. At seventy-eight, he was beginning to look fragile to her, despite her knowing he had a will of iron. He was too thin, a little stooped, and the face under a shock of white hair bore a road map of his hard life. He always said Audrey had been responsible for his getting old before his time. Lately, he'd been blaming Tansy, as well.

Rheumy eyes squinting, he looked around in vain. "You find the girl?"

"I found her. We had a disagreement. A good ride'll cool her off."

"More like her mama every day," he muttered darkly, setting himself down in the swing.

Willow supposed she could understand his disappointment in his only child. Audrey Kane had birthed two daughters out of wedlock by two different men, neither of whom he'd had the fortune to meet. Then one day, she'd up and left him with the burden of two young girls to raise, and all because of what he called

her reckless ways. He'd done his duty by them,
though, even loved them in his own crusty way. Too
damn proud to show it much, she guessed. Or maybe
he figured he'd get his heart broken all over again if he
acted too human. For whatever he said about their
mama, Willow sensed the love tainted by an old man's
bitterness.

"One day, she'll just ride off and never come back,"
he predicted. "Not until she needs something."

And Willow knew he was thinking about Mama.

"I better get inside and start supper. You have a
preference between chicken and fish tonight?"

"What's wrong with a good piece of red meat?" he
grumbled. "Why do we raise cattle if we can't eat
'em?"

She wasn't going to get in an argument over his
cholesterol again. "Because they pay the bills. Chicken
or fish?"

"I used to like chicken before you started skinning
it."

"Then I'll make the fish."

He grumped at her and waved her off.

While she got together rice and black beans and a
nice piece of grilled fish, she thought about Grandpa
Jonah's prediction. Worry ate at her insides. Surely
Tansy would never really leave her like Mama had, for
losing her sister would truly break her heart.

The seed was sown, though, and grew throughout
a silent dinner. No Tansy. Afterward, with Grandpa
staring at the television from his recliner, Willow tried
to read a magazine about ranching. Some time later,
she realized she was on the same article she'd started
with and hadn't the faintest idea of what lay on those
slick pages.

And still no Tansy.

The hour was late and Willow was feeling sick inside.

She called Mama, who, sounding properly concerned, said she hadn't seen her younger daughter. Willow's hand shook as she replaced the receiver in its cradle.

"Go to bed!" Grandpa ordered. "What's done is done. No help for it now."

"She'll come home," Willow said with more confidence than she was feeling. "She just wants to worry us."

Before she left the room, she swore she saw tears well in the old man's eyes.

Fighting tears herself, Willow lay in her lonely bed, staring up into the dark, hour after hour, listening for hoofbeats. While the night remained still, a presage of danger gripped her in its smothering grasp. She rose before dawn, meaning to take out her horse and find Tansy herself. She dressed quickly, then headed for the kitchen where she filled a canteen of water.

"You going after the girl?" came a voice from behind her.

Startled, she whirled around and picked out her grandpa's silhouette. "What are you doing, sitting there in the dark?"

"Couldn't sleep."

So he'd been worried, as well. He was still in his recliner, so it seemed he hadn't even gone to bed. She tried to cheer him up.

"Maybe Madrid threw a shoe or something and she's walking him home. I'll find her." When she got no reaction, she added, "This isn't like Mama."

"I hope not. If you're not back in a coupla hours, though, I'm calling the sheriff's office."

Willow swallowed hard but didn't discourage him.

A quarter of an hour later, with dawn on the horizon, she was well on her way, riding Tequila, an Appaloosa that she'd hand raised. In addition to the canteen of water, she'd taken along two saddlebags—one filled with emergency supplies including a first-aid kit, the other with food. The leather sheath attached to the saddle cradled a loaded rifle, the one along her hip, a knife. A rope looped around the saddle horn. She was prepared for anything.

As the sun rose, Willow easily picked up Madrid's tracks heading toward Mesa Milagro, a huge plateau of copper-tinted rock that dominated the area and sat at the eastern edge of their property. On the way, she passed the original two-room ranch house occupied by her ancestors, deserted now for half a century. Tracks told her Tansy had, indeed, been by here, but she'd gone on.

As did Willow.

The teenager had headed straight for the mesa, no doubt to what was left of the pueblo ruins that clung to a small cleft a hundred feet or so up. The knowledge gave Willow a measure of relief. The ruins, so like those of the ancient Anasazi rather than like more modern pueblos, were a favorite of Tansy's—a place where she went to be alone when something was troubling her. Her sister had always claimed the spot was magic. And even practical Willow couldn't disagree with her. She'd felt it, too, from the first time she'd set foot in the place as a kid.

Legend had it that in the late eighteenth century, when a clan of Pueblo Indians were trapped by an army of Spaniards with no way out, doomed to thirst and starvation if not violent death, they gathered inside the Great Kiva, their sacred space, and prayed to their gods to keep them safe... then simply vanished, never to be seen again.

Hence the superstitious, extremely religious Spaniards named the mesa *Milagro,* which meant miracle in Spanish.

With the rising sun beaming over its flat top, the mesa did look like magic. Afire, the rock glowed a deep copper, and as she stared at it, Willow had an unsettling feeling she couldn't put a name to.

"C'mon, Tequila."

Pressing her heels into the horse's sides, she urged him to go faster. Instinct told her that something wasn't right. Upon reaching the cliff's foot below the ruins, she found Madrid tethered in the shelter of a cottonwood stand that grew alongside a shallow ribbon of water trickling down from the mesa itself. A thread of relief coursed through Willow. Her imagination had been overheated. Of course her sister was here somewhere, just as she had suspected.

But when she called, "Tansy, where are you?" and got no reply, she couldn't stop her pulse from fluttering weirdly. Her words bounced off the striated rock and whispered through her, all lonely and scared sounding.

Stomach knotting, she dismounted wearily and checked over Madrid. Tansy had removed his saddle and had left it at the foot of the cottonwood. Madrid himself was cool and dry to the touch, obviously not having been ridden since the day before.

"So where's your mistress?" she asked him.

Tansy's horse rolled his eyes, snorted and tossed his head.

And Willow had the oddest feeling that he was trying to tell her something. Ridiculous. He was an animal, for heaven's sake. It was this place. The myth of a miracle. The wind tossing itself off the mesa, chilling her despite the rising sun.

"Tansy!" she called again, staring up at the ruins. "Please answer me. I've been worried. Grandpa, too. You've made your point. Now come on down. Let's go home and talk about whatever's bothering you!"

But she was talking to herself.

The echo of her own voice wailing through her made Willow's flesh crawl. Or maybe it was the foreboding feeling that something was not right. Madrid was here, so Tansy had to be here, as well. And while Tansy had a quick temper and could be extremely hotheaded in her actions, she didn't have a mean bone in her body. She'd had more than enough time to cool off. She wouldn't not answer on purpose.

Something was wrong.

Willow didn't consider the possibility—she just *knew*. A knowledge that seared her. Fearing Tansy might have hurt herself, perhaps fallen while scrambling over the broken rock and was now lying up there, unconscious, she gathered Tequila's reins and started for the steep, snaking slope that would take her up to the ruins clinging to the side of the mesa. Exhausted, having had no sleep for more than twenty-four hours, she had to force her limbs to make the effort. Normally, she wouldn't require the horse to make the long, awkward climb, but if she had to carry Tansy down...

"Tansy, honey, if you can hear me, let me know where you are!" she called.

Not expecting an answer, Willow was not surprised when she got none. She hurried, Tequila's snort and the *clip-clop* of his hooves her only assurances that she wasn't totally alone on the mesa. By the time she reached the beginning of the rubble that signaled the old pueblo's ruins, she was sweating inside and out. Wet with fear. Her heart squeezed tight and her eyes stung. She braced herself for what she might find.

"Tansy?" she called. "Tansy, can you hear me?"

She quickly looked through the honeycomb of partial walls—and found nothing. She scrambled over broken rock, poked her head into shattered shells of homes abandoned for two centuries, inspected every inch of the ruins, but she found no sign of her sister. Her search ended at the hiddenmost part of the ruins, the kiva. She drew Tequila closer to her, hugged his neck for comfort.

Once, walls would have risen around her, and entrance would have been via a ladder through the roof, for kivas were subterranean according to ritual. Stepped altars and rock ledges would have surrounded her. Now all that was left was the mesa wall itself, some crumbling indications of where the outside walls had been, and the shallow, navel-like notch of the *sipapu,* symbolic of the place where humans emerged from the earth. The *sipapu* also gave spiritual access to another world deeper below.

Below...

Willow's stomach clutched. "Tansy!" she yelled. "Are you down there?"

No answer came from the dark gaping maw. She opened one of her saddlebags and grabbed a flashlight. Sliding onto her stomach, she shone it into the rubble-filled chamber probably eight feet below.

Empty. Of human life, anyway. Who knew what desert creatures took shelter in the dark cavern?

No Tansy.

Willow flipped over and pushed herself the few feet to the rock wall so she could rest her back. She was tired. So very tired. Fatigue filled her, eroding any desire to search further for the moment. She couldn't think. Maybe if she rested for a while...

"Tequila, here," she called, following the verbal request by a sharp whistle.

The horse responded immediately, lumbering to her side. She picked up the dragging reins, secured them around a loose rock next to her. Discouraged, exhausted, heartsick, she settled back, thinking she merely needed a few minutes of rest to renew her spirit.

"Atta boy. Just let me get a second wind." Her eyelids fluttered. "We have to find her, Tequila. We have to find Tansy." She closed her eyes and, though she didn't much believe in miracles, prayed for one harder than she'd ever prayed for anything in her life. "Please let me find Tansy safe. And soon. No matter where she might be."

And then she allowed herself to drift...

...feeling as if she were suspended in time, imagined she sensed the heartbeats of her father's ancestors as they gathered around the sacred kiva, took comfort in their presence, became one with them, her prayer seeming a collective plea...

...awakening when the sun shone so strongly she could not deny its power. The golden orb hung low in the west, its brilliance casting a red glow over everything in its path.

Willow sat up with a start. She'd been sleeping for hours!

"Oh, Tansy, I didn't mean to desert you," she murmured, scrambling to her feet.

The world spun crazily and she hung on to Tequila's saddle until everything righted. She felt lightheaded. Different somehow. She'd gotten to her feet too quickly. She took a few deep breaths, replaced the flashlight and untied the horse's reins, then led the way out.

"Let's get going before the sun sets." Snaking her way back down to the high desert floor, she talked to Tequila to comfort herself. "We'll go back where Tansy left her horse and look for boot prints. Maybe she didn't come up here at all."

Though surely her sister wouldn't have gone so far that she couldn't hear Willow's call.

But Willow didn't know what to think when she found Madrid gone. "Tansy!" she screamed in frustration, wondering if her sister had heard her and had sneaked away behind her back. Furious with herself for letting down her guard, she yelled at the top of her lungs. "Tansy Kane, if you can hear me, you come back!"

Tequila whinnied nervously and danced away from her. Willow hardly noticed. She was staring at the ground. At the unfamiliar prints made by a strange horse. Shoes worn by the Rancho Milagro stock bore a special marking, a combined *R* and *M,* the ranch's brand. No such marking in the earth. But that was impossible. She looked harder.

And if she hadn't known better she'd swear Madrid had never been there.

A chill shot through her and she snugged a shoulder against Tequila for the animal's warmth. He, too, was quivering as if his nerves were itching. Her sister's horse had been here mere hours ago. So where were his prints?

Leading Tequila to drink at the stream before setting off for home, Willow noticed and then closely inspected some human boot prints around the damp earth. She distinguished two sets. One belonged to a large man. The other set was shorter and narrower. Tansy's? Both people had ridden off on the single horse.

Puzzled, mounting Tequila, Willow followed the tracks leading away from the stream. She'd gone maybe a quarter of a mile when something shiny in the sand caught her eye. She flew from Tequila's back to retrieve the object—the hair clasp Tansy had been wearing when she'd ridden off the day before!

So Tansy *had* been the second rider.

Not understanding how Madrid had disappeared without a trace or why her sister would ride off with some stranger, Willow tucked the hair clasp into a back pocket, then threw herself up into her saddle, determined to play catch-up before dark. She pinned her gaze to the ground, followed the tracks long enough to ride off Rancho Milagro and onto government land, every so often glancing up and searching the distance for any sign of life.

Eventually, a curious sight met her eyes.

Several cowboys and horses were gathered beneath a cottonwood. One man seemed to be struggling, as if trying to get away from the others. His hands were secured behind his back. Two men on foot threw him up onto a palomino with a burnished bronze coat and pewter mane and tail. Another mounted man drew closer, and Willow swore that looked like a rope in his hand. Squinting hard, she realized all of the cowboys wore bandannas covering their faces…all but the one who was fighting having a noose strung around his neck.

A hanging?

Thinking for a moment that she'd run into some kind of Wild West reenactment—they'd become awfully popular with the tourists—or perhaps a movie being shot, Willow looked around as she drew closer.

No audience. No camera crew.

And from the way the bound man was struggling…

Heart thundering in her breast, the truth sluicing through her—the man would be killed unless someone intervened—Willow freed her rifle and dug in her heels. Tequila shot forward as she yelled, "You, there! Stop!"

But either the masked men were so intent on their purpose they didn't hear her…or they were purposely ignoring her. She could see the noose tighten around the victim's neck and him stretching up in his saddle. He was saying something to the man who'd strung him up.

"Let him go before I shoot!" she yelled in warning.

The next thing Willow knew, the biggest of the men on foot slapped the palomino's rump. A sick feeling filling her, she stopped Tequila and shouldered her rifle, even as the palomino shot forward, heedless of the victim's desperate attempt to cling to the mare. The weight of his body jerked downward and his feet did a wild midair dance.

Sweat popping on her neck and brow, Willow got a bead high on the rope that was swinging with the hanged man's weight. Praying for accuracy, she squeezed the trigger, and the blast of her rifle jerked the vigilantes' heads around even as the rope split and the man dropped.

Too late?

Rope trailing in the dust, the hanged man lay still on the ground, while his horse pounded toward her and one of the masked men drew his gun.

Chapter Two

Without thinking about what she was doing, Willow reacted, shooting the gun out of the man's hand before he finished aiming at her.

"Next time, it won't be a gun!" she warned the others, heart thumping against her ribs as she wondered if they could hear the lie in her words. She couldn't actually shoot a person, for heaven's sake.

Never removing her eyes from the men, Willow used her legs to guide Tequila. The masked men blocked the downed man's horse from launching past them. Snorting, the palomino turned and slowed, coming to a short stop a few yards away.

"Who the hell do you think you are?" one of the masked men was demanding.

He was the big man who'd smacked the palomino—probably the leader of this vile group of men, Willow figured.

"A law-abiding citizen," she told him.

"Well this 'ere bastard is a murderer!"

A wave of unease shot through her. "That's for the law to decide . . . and a jury of his peers."

"You Smith's new woman?"

"Yeah, look at her. Dressed like some kinda man."

Realizing the man they'd tried to hang was writhing on the ground, Willow ignored their speculations. She indicated the only mounted vigilante, the hangman. "Off your horse, cowboy. Get rid of the rope and help him up."

Reluctantly, the vigilante did as she demanded. Willow kept a keen eye on them all, even when she edged Tequila over to the palomino and gathered the mare's reins. A light sweat coated her outside and fear made her insides tighten. They were armed, every one of them, handguns in holsters and rifles at their saddles. She was used to seeing an occasional cowboy likewise armed—in addition to rattlers, rustlers weren't unknown on the range even today—but a passel of them? Having an impromptu necktie party?

Willow felt as if she'd stepped through some time warp.

Drawing closer to the man named Smith, she got her first real look at the victim as he choked in some air. Or maybe the man was no victim, but a murderer. A real desperado.

Whichever, he was a handsome devil with burnished gold hair and a contrasting dark mustache. Kind of reminded her of Robert Redford playing the Sundance Kid in that old movie. A real fancy man, he was dressed like he should be in a movie, too, with an embroidered vest and ruffled shirt beneath his dust-laden black jacket that hung open to his hips, past his gun belt and empty holster.

"Release his hands," she added for good measure, aware of the accused murderer's piercing blue eyes trying to stare a hole through her. "The rest of you, drop your guns where you stand, then get over there," she said, using her rifle to indicate a spot away from their mounts.

Smith reached out for the hangman who'd just released him and grabbed a pearl-handled gun the vigilante had tucked into the waist of his denims. With a fancy twirl of the gun around his finger, he snugged the weapon in his own holster.

Not having missed the easy display, Willow waited until they'd all complied before tossing Smith the palomino's reins. "Better get on quick before one of 'em figures out *I'm* not a killer."

Still saying nothing, Smith flashed her another searing look and stepped up into a stirrup. As he threw the other leg over the saddle, Willow rushed the vigilantes' horses and fired her rifle into the air. She rode straight through the small band, scattering them, then was hard-pressed to avoid the leader who leaped at her. She threw out a booted foot that landed square in the middle of his chest.

He fell to his knees cursing her. "You'll regret that, you sorry-ass breed!"

Willow closed her ears against the cruel taunt, one she hadn't heard applied to herself since she was a kid. New Mexico was a melting pot for Anglos and Hispanics and Indians and every conceivable combination thereof. Not many people even took note of her mixed heritage. Shaking inside, she slid her rifle into its sheath.

"Get outta here!" she yelled at Smith, then rode fast without a look back.

She heard him, though, thundering after her. A glance over her shoulder assured her the vigilantes were hotfooting it for their horses and would be after them in minutes. And Smith was staring grimly at her.

Only then did she realize what danger she might have put herself in. What if the fancy man was a murderer? He might kill her for Tequila and her rifle and what she had in her saddlebags. Or maybe he'd be grateful and leave her alone, just hightail it out of the county while the going was good.

But at the moment, her bigger worry was that masked posse. If they caught her . . . though, having scattered their horses, she and Smith had such a head start, she hadn't even seen the men's dust.

It wasn't until they'd gone some distance and wound around a few hills that she slowed, heading Tequila across a rock-strewn slope toward the hidden mouth of a small box canyon. What next? The sun had set, the hills casting deep shadows around them. Smith was following her close enough to make her feel his presence.

She glanced over her shoulder. He rode tall in the saddle. Tall and silent. Not so much as a thank-you passed his pretty lips. But his eyes were a different story. They were talking to her, all right. Asking questions she didn't want to ask herself. Making her increasingly nervous.

She led the way behind a tumble of boulders that cleverly hid the entrance to the canyon. Somehow, the area looked a bit different, both the numbers of rocks and the vegetation, but she chalked that up to not having been here in quite a while, maybe a year or better.

At the yawning mouth of the canyon, Willow stopped and turned Tequila so she was facing Smith directly. "You can hide in here till you think they've given up."

"What about you?"

The words were whispered and forced and rough enough to make her realize why he hadn't said anything until now. Where the noose had decorated it, his neck was bruising purple. Undoubtedly his throat was swollen inside, making talking difficult.

Thinking some water would help, she released her canteen and offered it to him. "Here. Drink."

He took the leather strap from her, his long fingers brushing hers in the process. In that short moment, something startling and intense passed between them. Willow whipped her hand away, but couldn't do the same with her wide-eyed gaze. She watched him take his fill of the water. He threw his golden head back and gulped, and she could see a nasty rope burn on his throat in addition to the bruising. He passed the canteen back to her, and she was careful to keep the trade impersonal.

"What about you?" he asked again, his voice a bit stronger, if still rough.

She secured the canteen to her saddle. "I can take care of myself."

"Not with those varmints running loose around the countryside, you can't!" Smith protested vehemently. "Considering what you did for me, they'd just as soon string you up as look at you cross-eyed...."

He hesitated long enough to give her another of those searing looks. One that made Willow's mouth go dry and her pulse pound.

"...after having some fun with you first," he finished flatly.

The implication negated the powerful effect he was having on her, while the thought of such an unspeakable thing happening to her made Willow's head go light. She swayed in her saddle. Smith moved toward her. Before she had time to react, he'd snatched Tequila's reins directly under the horse's mouth, effectively taking away her control. He led her straight into the canyon. She should have fought him, should have ripped the reins from his hand, turned tail and made a run for it, but for the first time the folly of what she'd done sank in.

Forgetting all about Tansy for a while, she'd acted totally out of character. A woman who'd never before had an adventurous moment in her life, she'd spent the last half hour riding to the rescue of a stranger, shooting the gun from a man's hand, and taking off like a bat out of hell!

What in the world had gotten into her?

Now she had three nasty-tempered, lawless men seeing-red angry with her. And she didn't know which was the worse of two evils—facing them down, or being alone with this handsome desperado.

This possible murderer.

So when Smith dismounted and grabbed her around the waist, pulling her from her horse, Willow panicked and struck out at him, legs flailing, hands going straight for his face.

HAVING PUT UP with about as much as any man could for one day, Ryder was not about to let the wildcat end his future possibilities for fatherhood or let her mark his face. Then again, he didn't want to hurt the person who'd saved his hide. He chose the only possible solution, pulling her straight toward him and flipping them both around so she was trapped between him and the canyon's wall. Her hat flew off and he got his first real good look at her.

Her widened eyes were a luminous light brown. In contrast, her lashes were a sooty black like the thick waist-length hair that fell over one shoulder in a braid. Her cheekbones were high, her jaw square, her mouth ripe, her skin naturally sun kissed. She *was* part Indian—not that it mattered to him. More importantly, she reminded him just a little of Ramona, if a more mature and stunning version of the comely saloon girl, and the strange coincidence gave him a start.

Feeling foolish that his head was doing this weird dance on him, able to feel the jagged pounding of his deliverer's heart against his chest, Ryder groused, "What the hell's wrong with you, lady?" then regretted letting so many words out of his mouth at once. His throat felt like raw meat inside.

"I don't like being mauled."

"This isn't mauling." Though he was pressed up tight against her.

"Then what do you call it?"

"Self-protection."

Her full mouth gaped before she was able to respond. "Against *me?*"

"You *are* the same woman who got the draw on three men to rescue me, aren't you?" he asked caustically. "You split a hangman's rope in two and shot a gun out of a man's hand without so much as flinching."

A flush darkened her golden skin. "I—I was just acting on instinct, is all."

He'd like to act on instinct. If anyone would have told him he could be aroused within the hour of feeling the hangman's noose around his neck, he'd have called him crazy. But here he was, need mounting faster than he'd ever have imagined. Her woman's softness and distinctive smell were more appealing than they should be—considering Ramona was hardly cold in her grave. Still, proof of his arousal pressed into her belly. And he was certain she knew it. She was shaking slightly, and he recognized fear deep in those translucent brown eyes, though her expression remained defiant.

Cursing himself, he backed off some, if not enough to let her escape. "Didn't mean to scare you none."

"Well you did. This whole thing scared me. A vigilante hanging in 1995—who would have thought it possible?"

Ryder started. "You *are* shook up. You mean 1885."

"No, of course I don't!" she snapped, her hands flat against his chest and pushing. "Though considering what happened today, it *should* be 1885."

He didn't let her budge him. "It *is* 1885."

That lovely mouth gaped again, and Ryder was hard-pressed not to act on the instinct to taste it. Yet something about her seriousness, about the way she was looking at him as if he were crazy, put him off. She was the one who seemed to be touched in the head. He'd known a woman like that once, back in Kansas City. Had delusions, Maggie did, though hers had been of a carnal nature, near impossible to resist.

Grinning at the fond remembrance, he stepped back and took a better look at this one's apparel—pants, shirt, vest, well-worn, hand-tooled leather boots. "Uh, you do know you're a woman, right?"

"I beg your pardon?"

"Well, you *are* dressed in men's clothing."

Gaze narrowing, she asked, "What century are you living in, bub?"

Bub? "Like I said, the nineteenth."

The mouth gaped yet again before a disbelieving, "Uh-huh," passed those luscious lips.

She was staring at him warily now. Ryder felt the short hairs at the back of his neck rise, and a chill shot down his spine. Something weird was going on here. Something out of his experience. But before he could press her for further explanation, she distracted him by skirting around him and proceeding toward her Appaloosa.

"Where do you think you're hightailing it to?"

"To look for my sister, which I should have been doing this last hour."

Knowing Cal Atchley's boys could still be out there, certain they wouldn't be any more charitable to her than they'd been to him, Ryder didn't think her leaving was a wise idea. And she had saved his miserable hide.

He grabbed her arm and spun her around. "Better to stay here till after dark."

Which wouldn't be long. The sun had set and the gray of dusk washed over the canyon. Still, she seemed torn. Ryder could tell she was itching to get away from him.

"I'm not going to hurt you." Unable to keep the disgust from his hoarse voice, he released his grip on her arm. "You have my solemn word on it."

"The word of...an accused murderer, Mr. *Smith?*"

She had starch, he'd give her that. But she wasn't unafraid. He didn't miss the irregular pulse beating in her throat or the odd inflection she gave his name. As if there weren't a whole bunch of people named Smith in this part of the country.

"Name's Ryder," he said truthfully. "And I was falsely accused, not rightfully convicted."

She stared at him as if trying to read through his eyes and right into his very soul. If he still had one. Ryder imagined he was already damned for all time.

Finally, seeming satisfied, she nodded. "Then let me get some food from my saddlebag. And I have a first-aid kit. I can fix up your neck."

But Ryder wasn't eager to have anyone touch the abused flesh. "You can damn well leave my neck alone!"

"And let it get infected?" She shrugged. "Up to you."

He narrowed his gaze at her. "You one of them lady doctors or something?"

"No. A rancher. Over the years, I've had plenty of reason to learn something about patching up a man." When he didn't immediately agree, she arched her eyebrows. "Unless you're afraid, of course."

Not one to let some woman think she intimidated him, Ryder growled, "Get what you need."

Though he had cause to regret his good nature a short while later after they'd tied up the horses and she was applying something she called hydrogen peroxide to the raw flesh. In addition to making the rope burn feel like it was on fire, the solution sizzled, making him wonder if she was using some kind of witchcraft on him.

"It'll feel better as soon as it dries," she assured him, replacing the odd top to the small bottle. "It'll cool down. Then I'll put some Neosporin ointment on it."

Ryder looked at the bottle as she replaced it in her kit. But it was her hands that really fascinated him.

She had gentle hands, he'd give her that, and yet he'd felt the rough calluses that gave truth to her statement about working as a rancher. Had her family died and left her a spread? Could be a spinster. Or maybe she was a widow.

"What name do you go by?"

"Willow Kane."

"Willow. Pretty."

"My father named me. Or so Mama told me."

"Who gave you the Kane part?" he asked casually—for all he knew she could be a properly married woman.

From what he could still see in the near dark, her jaw tightened a bit. "That part came from Mama."

Ryder didn't miss her meaning. Nor did he miss the fact that she wasn't married.

Willow spread the ointment on his neck, her movements hasty. If he didn't hurt so damn bad, he'd suggest she slow down some, let those rough fingertips linger a bit on his flesh. He was a mite disappointed when she finished and packed her kit back into her saddlebag.

"I have some food. I can leave you some."

"You can stay and share a meal with me instead." Sensing her reluctance and averse to losing her company, he said, "I *insist.*"

"I need to get going. I have to find my sister."

"It's dark."

"Which makes Tansy's continued absence even more scary," Willow said, sounding more and more tense with each sally. "This is the second night she's out here somewhere on her own."

"Maybe she went home on her own while you were looking for her."

"I don't know...I only hope Grandpa Jonah called the sheriff like he meant to." Sounding hopeful, she said, "Maybe they already found Tansy."

As if Sheriff Landry would look for a missing girl when he was doing nothing about the one who'd just been murdered, Ryder thought, deciding it would be wise to withhold that observation.

"Then there's no reason you have to hurry off." Though he could tell Willow wasn't swayed, she didn't come back at him with another argument. Grinning at the minor victory, he said, "You fetch that grub and I'll see if I can't find something to get a fire going. We can talk about your sister over supper."

A short silence was followed by her tight, "Fine. You want to use my flashlight?"

"Your what?"

"My flash..." She gave him a wary look and backed up. "Uh, never mind."

Though she sounded and was acting mighty peculiar, Ryder shrugged and went about his business, finding a few pieces of usable wood and depositing them in a pile. He glanced back to see what Willow was about, but he could barely make out her movements by the light of the moon. She was digging into her saddlebags. But when he was crouched to gather dried twigs and branches for kindling, he heard her come up behind him a bit too stealthily for his peace of mind. He quickly turned his head and looked straight into a strange, bright light that blinded him and froze him to the spot.

Ryder sensed rather than actually saw Willow's quick movement as she muttered, "I'm really sorry you forced me to do this."

Suddenly his head exploded with bright lights...
then the lights went out in a dizzying rush.

APPALLED BY her own violent action, Willow watched
Ryder Smith crumple at her feet and got a good look
at the blood streaking the gold threads of his hair. She
ran the flashlight beam over him. He was unconscious, but she caught the slight movement of his
chest. Thank goodness, he was breathing. Her sky-
rocketing pulse steadied, and she dropped the piece of
firewood she'd used as an impromptu weapon. She
hadn't wanted to hurt the man—certainly would never
have shot him—but he'd been so bound and determined to keep her with him, was so much stronger
than she, that she'd had to do *something* to get away.

She had to find out if Tansy was home.

Whirling, Willow headed for Tequila and mounted
him on the run, shoving the flashlight into the saddlebag behind her. She'd left the unconscious man
food—as if that would appease him when he woke
with a throbbing head. A moment later, she was free
of the canyon and the vexing Ryder Smith.

Truth be told, the stranger was disturbing to her on
more than one level. He was an accused murderer.
One who insisted she was in the wrong century. And
one to whom she was undeniably attracted.

Attracted to a screwy, possibly dangerous, if good-
looking, man, Willow chided herself.

She had to get out more often.

Traveling by instinct, with a little help from the
stars, she headed back to Rancho Milagro as fast as
she dared. She wasn't about to let Tequila break a leg
in some snake hole, and so it was a while before she
came in sight of the original ranch house. On a small

rise above it, she stopped and stared in shock. The
windows were lit and smoke wafted out the chimney,
giving the place a lived-in appearance.

"Tansy, is that where you've been?"

Eagerly, Willow guided Tequila downhill. But as she
circled around to the front, she drew up short while
still some distance away. Tied to the hitching post were
three newly familiar horses—a paint, a roan and a
dun—ones she'd seen only a few hours before. The
vigilantes were inside. With her sister?

Panicked, she tied Tequila to a juniper bush, slid her
rifle from its sheath and started to creep toward the
house. She stopped in her tracks at the sound of male
voices.

"Sorry to disturb you," the vigilante leader was
saying as he and his men exited.

Willow backed up and took shelter next to the
horse.

A man she hadn't seen before stepped out onto the
porch after them. "No bother." The light from the
house haloed him—tall, muscular, long black hair.
"I'll keep an eye out for this Ryder Smith," he promised, his tone deadly serious.

"Watch out for his woman," the hangman warned.
"She's as mean tempered and dangerous as he is."

"I'll do that," the stranger agreed, his dead-serious
tone lightening a bit.

As Willow considered how funny it was that they
thought *she* was dangerous, the vigilantes rode off.
The stranger stared after them for a moment, and
though Willow stood perfectly still, her hand over Tequila's nose, the man turned his face her way as if he
sensed their presence. She could see his imposing silhouette through the bushes because of the light com-

ing from the house, but she assumed he couldn't pick her or her horse out by moonlight, as well camouflaged as they were. Still, a thrill of fear shot through Willow until he finally backed off and entered the house, closing the door behind him.

Another problem for the sheriff to handle. They'd never had a squatter on their property before.

Willow waited awhile before attempting to leave, not wanting another unexpected run-in. The house looked quiet. She untied Tequila and led him away. All she wanted to do was get home to find that Tansy had beat her there. She wanted to make peace with her sister. Further worrying about vigilantes and squatters could wait until morning.

But when Willow looked back, another chill shot down her spine.

On the other side of the old house, two horses were grazing in a corral...where no corral had stood for as long as she could remember. Then again, perhaps he'd built the simple split-rail enclosure when he'd made himself at home in the long-abandoned building. It was possible, Willow told herself, considering she hadn't been by the place in weeks. She also supposed the corral could have been there that morning and she just hadn't noticed.

Anxiously, Willow rode for home...chest tightening when she arrived at the valley and found it empty. A sick feeling in her stomach, she looked around for the house.

No house.

No barn.

No bunkhouse.

No corral.

No toolshed.

What the hell was going on?

Willow refused to imagine the unthinkable. She rode in circles for at least another hour before deciding that the night had her all confused. So much had happened in so short a time. She needed food and a good rest, was all. Trying not to panic, she took shelter in a familiar spot—an underhang that she'd used a couple of times as a kid to protect her from spring rains. She removed Tequila's leathers, except for his halter, to which she tied the rope that she then secured to a tree. Finally, she forced herself to eat what food she hadn't left for Ryder.

She wouldn't panic. Everything would be back to normal in the morning...

...only it wasn't.

Even under a brilliant blue sky, Willow found no trace of the house she'd lived in half her life. All had simply disappeared. Unbelievable. Impossible. Had she gone crazy? She rode southeast in the general direction of Santa Fe. She should have passed another ranch house. Barns. Paved roads. A bingo palace on a neighboring pueblo. A highway. A housing development at the edge of town.

Only she didn't.

Mile after mile, across rock and plain and *arroyo,* she crossed familiar terrain dotted with horses or cattle, but with not a single man-made landmark that she recognized.

Only later, on a hill overlooking Santa Fe, did she come to terms with her waking nightmare. All the newer neighborhoods and motels and restaurants had vanished, leaving the old city snugged around the plaza and Fort Marcy. The streets were dirt, the vehicles horses and carriages, the Agua Fria lined with farms rather than adobe homes.

Ryder Smith hadn't been demented, after all. This *was* 1885.

Either that, or *she* was crazy.

She felt like Dorothy in *The Wizard of Oz* after the tornado.

Mentally exhausted and heartsick, fearing that she would see neither Tansy nor Grandpa Jonah nor Mama ever again, Willow tied Tequila to a hitching post and stumbled into a newly whitewashed Santuario de Guadelupe, seeking solace. The interior was cool, thanks to its three-foot-thick adobe walls with small windows, and a high ceiling adorned by fine, old, carved *vigas* and corbels. The church was a bit shabbier than she remembered it, but it had gone through a recent renovation.

That is, recent to 1995.

Lost, she sat before the statue of Our Lady of Guadelupe at a side altar and prayed for help. Prayed for some way out of this nightmare.

"What's troubling you, my child?" rumbled a smooth, if elderly, voice from behind her.

Eyes filled with tears, Willow whipped around to see a white-haired priest in a black cossack hovering at a respectful distance—far enough away so she didn't feel overwhelmed by his presence. Without even trying, he encouraged her to tell the truth, no matter how weird it might sound. Still, she chose her words carefully, lest she be committed to some asylum.

"I don't belong in this place or time, Father. I don't know how I got here...don't know how to get back where I belong. What am I going to do?"

The priest stepped closer, his expression kindly. "Many of our Lord's flock are lost, my child. But He works in mysterious ways. Perhaps He brought you to a strange land for a purpose."

"What purpose?"

"That is for you to decide..."

To find Tansy.

"...and for you to make the most of your opportunity," he finished.

Willow remembered praying at the kiva that she would find Tansy no matter where she had to go, what she had to do...just as the Pueblo Indians that inhabited the site must have done two hundred years before to get away from the Spaniards who trapped them. Perhaps the clan's strange disappearance wasn't merely legend. Perhaps they, too, had prayed hard enough to vanish from their time.

Everything started coming together then. Ryder Smith. The vigilantes. Her sister's horse being gone.

The hair clip she'd found!

"Thank you, Father. You've opened my eyes."

Or, rather, her mind. She'd found Tansy's silver-and-green-turquoise clip *after* leaving the kiva. Therefore, she could assume her sister had slipped through the same crack in time that she had. Tansy was crazy about this period in New Mexico's history—compliments of all those dreadful Wolf Madrid dime novels. If her sister had wished herself away, Willow was certain it would be to the here and now.

"I have done nothing more than listen, my child," the priest murmured. "But if you need an attentive ear again, you will find me here."

"I'll remember that."

And perhaps she would see him again, Willow thought, for she wasn't about to figure out how to return to the present until she searched the past for her little sister!

Chapter Three

Willow spent the better part of the day working her way across Santa Fe, traipsing in and out of businesses and asking after Tansy, which proved to be an exercise in frustration. No leads and several cold shoulders later—undoubtedly because she was wearing men's clothing, added to her being part *Injun*, as she'd heard one man mutter to his companion—she decided she needed to do something about Tequila.

The poor horse appeared as exhausted as she was feeling. He'd had water and had grazed on sparse range grass, but he'd had no grain in nearly two days. She spotted a stable of jacal construction—squared-off cedar logs set upright in the ground, cracks chinked with adobe, and a sod roof.

"How long you need the stall?" the stable owner asked when she turned over Tequila's reins.

A slender, darkly handsome man in his late twenties, Miguel Borrego had an oddly arresting gaze. His near-black eyes boring into her made Willow shift uncomfortably.

"I'm not certain." For less than a day if she had her way, but she wasn't betting that finding Tansy would be so easy. "Can we keep the arrangement open?"

Borrego nodded. "You pay once a week on Saturdays."

"Saturday," she echoed, wondering how many days that gave her. In 1995, today would be Thursday.

A more important consideration was how she was going to come up with the money for Tequila's keep. Or her own, for that matter. Her twentieth-century currency was about as useful as Confederate bills after the Civil War, so she was grateful the stable owner hadn't demanded payment up front.

Feeling Borrego's eyes follow her—a spooky sensation that made the skin along her spine crawl—Willow shouldered her saddlebags and rifle and took off.

The fact that Tansy would have had to find a way to pay for room and board struck her. Or perhaps the girl was homeless, wandering the streets, trying to get a handout, sleeping in back alleyways and eating from the leavings of others.

Worry about her sister gnawing at her, Willow entered the plaza, which didn't look all that different from the present-day Santa Fe she knew so well . . . if she discounted the people in period clothing and the horse-drawn vehicles crowding the rutted dirt streets.

The Palace of the Governors—a long, seventeenth-century adobe building with a great portal and heavy wooden doors—dominated one side of the plaza, while shops and businesses lined the other three. And within the palace—a historical museum to her—the territorial offices of the government were housed. The U.S. Army had taken up headquarters in the buildings to the north, leaving barricaded Fort Marcy empty on its hill overlooking Santa Fe.

In place of the flank of Indians selling jewelry, leather goods, pottery and weavings that she was used

to seeing around the plaza, especially in front of the
Palace of the Governors, only a few Pueblos were
selling their wares. They set their blankets on rough-
board sidewalks beneath territorial-style wooden *por-
tales*—arcades or overhangs that sheltered the store-
fronts from the elements.

Standing near the gazebo in the middle of the
square, where civilians and soldiers alike strode by,
Willow scanned the myriad surrounding businesses.
The Whitiker General Store seemed to be the place
most likely to attract a teenager, so Willow decided to
start there.

Halfway across the street, she spotted a familiar
palomino heading straight for her. Pulse jagging, she
ran the last few yards, up and over the planked side-
walk to the open doorway. Noting the sign in the front
window—Titus and Velma Whitiker, Proprietor and
Wife, and a smaller, Est. 1885—she entered the new
store filled with everything from hardware to dry
goods.

Inside, wondering if she'd been spotted, she peered
through the plate-glass window, her heart in her
throat. Her tumult was due to caution and a healthy
bit of fear, Willow told herself, not to her attraction to
an accused murderer. If he caught up to her, how
would Ryder Smith exact revenge for that bump on his
head? But as he rode by, as tall in the saddle as ever,
she figured she might never know, since he didn't so
much as glance in her direction.

Thank goodness, Willow thought, leaning in close
to the glass and craning her neck. She watched him
until her view gave way.

She was just taking an easy breath, when from directly behind her came, "Can I help you, sir?" and she knew the woman was speaking to her.

"I sure hope so."

Willow turned and waited a beat for the woman's shock to settle. Undoubtedly this was Velma Whitiker, middle-aged with a thickening waist and graying brown hair. She was a comfortable-looking woman, even with her eyes wide and complexion pinkening, obviously from her embarrassment.

"I'm so sorry, miss!" Velma's fingers nervously pleated the material of her long skirts. She continued to stare. "I didn't mean no insult. Just that not many ladies are daring enough to wear men's trousers, even here in this godforsaken town."

Having been in one of the many churches in the area that very day, Willow thought *godforsaken* a bit of an exaggeration. But if the woman was new to the West, she was undoubtedly having a difficult time getting used to its rough ways. At least she wasn't turning her back on Willow as had many other people she'd come in contact with earlier.

"No need for an apology," she said graciously, adding a smile.

Velma Whitiker gave her a peculiar look, then took a big breath and asked, "So, what can I do for you?" though she still seemed uncomfortable.

"I'm looking for my younger sister, Tansy Kane. She's very pretty, has curly red hair and green eyes. She'd probably be dressed like I am. You might have seen Tansy around here yesterday or earlier today."

The woman was shaking her head before Willow even finished. "Haven't seen anyone like that ... I think I would have remembered."

Willow was certain Velma would, too. "Tansy might still come by here. If you do see her, would you give her a message—that her sister Willow is looking for her? I'll be back to check again, either later on today or tomorrow."

Velma Whitiker's expression continued to look perplexed. "Your little sister lost." She sucked in her plump cheeks. "*Tch-tch-tch.* A runaway?"

"Something like that."

"Oh, you poor thing. You must be going daft with worry. I did when our boy Pete up and left in the middle of the night." Voice strained, Velma added, "Thought his pa was too strict."

"Tansy thinks we're too strict...me and Grandpa."

With a smile at once sympathetic and strained, Velma said, "You look spent. How about some tea? I have some on the stove."

"That's very kind of you, but I can't pay." Not unless she wanted the woman to think she was nuts by trying to give her money dated a hundred years in the future.

"Charging you for a simple cup of tea wouldn't be very neighborly of me, now would it? Come."

Willow didn't hesitate. Wearier than she'd ever felt in her life, she could use not only tea and a temporary seat, but a bed for the night, as well. Maybe the shopkeeper could tell her where to find a safe and inexpensive shelter, otherwise, she might be spending the night with Tequila in his stall. She'd figure out some way to pay her way in trade.

At the back of the store, a teakettle sat upon a pot-bellied stove that overheated the cozy, private corner with its two chairs and tiny table. Even so, a shawl clung to the shoulders of Velma's long-sleeved green dress, as if she were perpetually cold.

Willow set down her saddlebags on the floor and braced her rifle on the wall next to the chair that Velma indicated she should take. Sitting felt so good. While the other woman poured hot water into a teapot, Willow fanned herself and looked around, not missing the canister of belladonna amidst the jars of tea leaves and herbs on the shelf. Also prominent was a fancily framed tintype of a long-haired young man who looked vaguely familiar.

Before Willow could ponder it, Velma asked, "So, where you from?" and placed the pot and two cups and saucers on the table. She was staring so hard, Willow shifted.

"Northwest."

Sitting, the woman looked surprised. "Really?"

"Our ranch is quite a ride from here," Willow hedged, for actually the distance wasn't so great, not even in 1885 when ranches covered thousands of acres and towns were few and far between.

"What's your spread?"

"Rancho Milagro."

Pouring their tea, Velma shrugged and said, "Must be quite a ways out. Never heard of it."

Which didn't surprise Willow, since her great-grandpa hadn't named it such until 1912, the year New Mexico became a state. Before Velma could continue with her questions, the front door slammed open, and a paunchy, middle-aged man burst through the door.

"Did you hear the news, woman?" he yelled, red faced all the way up into his thinning light brown hair.

Annoyance crossing her normally placid features, Velma called sweetly, "What news, Titus?"

"About Ryder…" he said, making Willow start just as she was about to take her first sip of tea. The man stalked his wife but faltered and stopped a yard from the table when he saw she wasn't alone. "I didn't realize we had a customer."

"This nice young woman is looking for her missing sister," Velma explained. "I offered her a bit of peace before she goes on."

Another man who'd followed Titus into the store called out, "Ya got any Old Kentucky tobacco, Titus?"

"Got a shipment last week, Caesar," the shopkeeper said, turning to the customer. "I'll get you some."

When he moved off behind the counter, Willow could see the other man. Recognition made her pulse jump. She swore this was the vigilante hangman, even though the last time she'd seen him, his face had mostly been hidden by a bandanna.

The man saw her, too. His pale blue eyes narrowed and his homely features twisted. "You!" he spat. "Titus, this is the woman I told you about. The no-account who freed Ryder Smith from getting his justice!"

The shopkeeper flew back around the counter and towered over Willow threateningly. "You freed that murdering varmint?"

Immediately edgy, Willow met his furious gaze. "I stopped some vigilantes from hanging a man who hadn't been arrested for a crime, yes."

"May God punish you for your sins to mankind!" he yelled.

Chilling Willow. "I'm sure he will. Only seeing that a man doesn't hang without having a fair trial first doesn't happen to be one of them."

"He killed that woman as sure as he—"

"Titus!" Velma cried. Whipping out of her seat, she exchanged a meaningful look with her husband and touched his arm soothingly. "Enough, please," she said in a soft voice.

The man acquiesced though his face was now close to being purple.

With a regretful glance at her still-full teacup, Willow rose. "I should get going."

"I'll keep an eye out for Tansy, just like you said," Velma promised, though her tone was a bit chilly.

The woman's expression had also changed. Closed. And she was looking at Willow more closely, as if she were inspecting some sort of oddity. Thinking Velma must believe Ryder was guilty of murder, also, Willow marveled at her restraint.

"Thank you for the tea, Velma."

Rifle and saddlebags in hand, Willow swept by a glowering Titus and met Caesar's gaze. As she passed by the hangman, his pale blue eyes were as still as death and fixed on her. Not a pretty invitation.

"Look to your back, woman," he muttered.

A chill followed her as she left the store.

And made her wonder if she'd made a mistake freeing Ryder Smith. But he'd come back to Santa Fe, Willow reasoned. Surely he wouldn't return to the scene of the crime if he was guilty. Not unless he had some incredible nerve.

He did have nerve, she remembered. And if he was a murderer, possibly he was itching for revenge against those who had tried to string him up.

Willow only *hoped* that revenge was saved for the vigilantes and that she was the last thing on his mind.

EVERYWHERE RYDER TURNED, he expected to see Miss Willow Kane.

Tracking her had been easy, what with that fancy marking that looked like a brand distinguishing her horse's prints. With a mind to catching up to her, he'd followed. He'd lost her for a while, then had picked up the tracks again. Convenient that they'd both been riding in the same direction. He'd lost her upon entering Santa Fe, but an ingrained intuition—the natural instinct that had kept him alive more than thirty years—told him he hadn't seen the last of the determined, gutsy woman.

At least he hoped that was the case, though he hadn't yet figured on how he was going to reward her for saving his hide, or how he would reprove her for the egg-size lump on his head. That'd teach him to turn his back on a woman whose sanity he'd already been questioning. 1995, indeed.

Still, Ryder couldn't say which he looked forward to more—the rewarding or the reproving.

Once through the plaza, he stabled his horse at Borrego's and walked along a *trazo*, a Spanish colonial town pattern. Each of the buildings had a *placita*, or interior courtyard with common walls that formed a continuous facade along the narrow street. He entered a nearby courtyard and crossed to the building's outside stairs, which he climbed to his rooms on the second floor. When he'd come to Santa Fe nearly a year ago, he'd rented this suite, the best in the house.

A while later, lying on his ornate canopy bed draped with heavy red material, he thought about the irony of his almost being hung now. He deserved it, of course. Had for years. No matter his protest, he was guilty. And one of these days, he would be served up his fitting punishment.

Ryder only wondered how much time he had left before true justice caught up to him.

HAVING CHECKED OUT the stores and other businesses in the plaza, Willow wearily started along another side street. When she came to the Red Mesa Saloon tucked behind a wall, she almost passed the place by, but something made her change her mind.

She crossed the pretty courtyard, with its cottonwood tree and flowering plants, and approached the main entrance. The walkway was tile, the building whitewashed adobe with blue trim. The owner must be superstitious. Even in present-day New Mexico, blue sashes and doorways were meant to keep out evil spirits. Some things never changed.

Inside, she looked around, her eyes taking a minute to adjust to the dim light, then registering dark wood and gaming tables, crystal chandeliers and a magnificent, hand-carved wooden bar with one of the largest antique mirrors she'd ever seen. The walls were a deep red. The place was empty but for a lone man with a bottle of whiskey at a corner table and a plump woman with dyed maroon hair setting out glasses behind the bar.

She approached the woman, who was dressed in a purple satin, low-cut dress. "Afternoon, I'm looking for—"

"Work? Just happens we have a recent vacancy."
The woman's limpid gray eyes swept over her with
approval. "Need a new pretty face to keep customers
coming in and spending money. You'll do."

Startled by the unexpected offer, Willow thought
quickly. She'd been wondering how she was going to
earn her keep until she could find Tansy. Besides, a
saloon would give her access to a lot of people, any of
whom might have seen her sister. This was perfect.

"I do need a job."

"Good. I'm Hazel Pruitt, owner of this fine establishment. Got any talent? Singing? Dancing?"

Willow eyed the small stage at the opposite end of
the room. "I'm afraid my talents are in the steer rop-
ing, sharpshooting categories." Her shoulders sagged
as she saw the job slipping away.

"Well, not all my girls are blessed with musical-
ity." The woman rolled her eyes and muttered,
"Though Rosabelle and Amabelle Nelson think they
are. Don't worry about it. We'll see how you do with
the customers."

"Then I have the job?"

"On a trial basis. I got a feeling the men who visit
my establishment are gonna like you right fine. Until
I decide whether or not you're gonna work out, you
get meals in the kitchen, a room upstairs, and as many
tips as you can wheedle out of your customers."

Customers...uh-oh. Willow realized what that
might mean. She wasn't that desperate. "You're not
saying I have to take those customers *upstairs*..."

Hazel raised her eyebrows. "That's up to you. I
don't run no bordello, but I understand a girl's gotta
make a living if she's ever gonna get ahead. I don't

pass judgment on what them who work for me do after hours, and I don't expect you to, either."

Willow couldn't help but wonder what Hazel might have had to do to buy the Red Mesa Saloon, although she was relieved that nothing untoward would be expected of her. "Fair enough."

"Then we got ourselves a deal. What'd you say your name was?"

Willow shook the hand the other woman offered. "Willow Kane."

Hazel indicated Willow's saddlebags. "You wouldn't have yourself something pretty to wear in there?"

"Afraid not."

"Figures. Well, you're gonna be using Ramona's old room. You might as well use her clothes. You're about the same size, if a mite taller."

Though Willow thought it odd the former saloon girl left behind clothing in an age when ready-to-wear wasn't too common in this part of the country, she didn't comment, merely followed Hazel upstairs and halfway down the red-flocked, wallpapered hall.

Her room was tiny with a narrow bed and a scarred dresser, upon which sat a bowl and pitcher for bathing and a Bible for cleansing of the soul. Several garments hung from pegs on the wall.

Willow threw her saddlebags and rifle onto the mattress. The springs squeaked. Hazel gave her possessions a curious look, which set Willow to sweating inside. While standard items in the Old West, both were updated versions, of course. But if the other woman took note of her modern rifle, she didn't comment.

Instead, she got down to practicalities. "The private is down the hall to the right. You can get supper in the kitchen at five. I expect you to be downstairs wearing your prettiest smile and something more suitable at six. That's when the customers start driftin' in."

"I won't be late." As the other woman turned to go, Willow said, "Hazel, I'm in town because I'm looking for my younger sister, Tansy. Pretty girl. Curly red hair. Green eyes. Sound familiar?"

"Honey, if I'd seen her, she'd already be working for me."

If only Tansy was getting a helping hand from someone as forthright as Hazel Pruitt. Willow shuddered to think of her sister in less scrupulous company.

"Should she wander in when I'm not downstairs, don't let her get away. Please."

The saloon owner's expression was sympathetic. "I'd give anything to get some time with my kin again, so I know how you feel. I'll let you know if I see anyone who fits that description."

"Thanks."

Hazel left and Willow checked her watch. Four o'clock. Enough time to rest a bit before going down for supper. Her stomach protesting the wait, she shoved over her rifle and saddlebags and sprawled across the thin, lumpy mattress.

Her watch.

Willow started.

Like the flashlight and a few other objects she was carrying with her, a wristwatch would be anachronistic in the nineteenth century.

Men owned pocket watches and women watches that pinned to their garments. And they certainly didn't have ones that ran on batteries or that glowed in the dark like hers did. She undid the catch and placed her wristwatch in a pocket, then decided she should store her other possessions under the bed so they wouldn't raise questions if someone else was to wander in. The key in the door lock didn't mean anything. She had a feeling total privacy was unlikely in a place like this.

Then, closing her eyes, she concentrated on Tansy, wishing the kiva's magic had come with her so she could transport herself into her sister's presence.

BUT WHEN WILLOW AWOKE a while later, she hadn't done more than roll over in her bed. Disappointed, she stumbled down to the kitchen for that supper. She was late so she ate alone. The Mexican cook kept giving her odd looks as she wolfed down her food. Then, stomach appeased, Willow returned to her room to change.

She chose the most modest of the outfits Ramona had left behind—a deep green skirt and a white *camisa,* an off-the-shoulder blouse with ruffles.

Oddly enough, she jingled as she moved around the room and, upon investigation, discovered Ramona had sewn a handful of coins into her petticoats. All the small cent and five-cent pieces had tiny holes drilled above Lady Liberty's head, through which the coins were sewn to the cloth. Defacing coins wasn't exactly legal, but she doubted anyone would care out here. She smoothed her skirts in place, thinking the jingling coins were Ramona's nest egg.

That made Willow feel weird. Why would any woman go off and leave not only her clothes, but her money? Had something happened to Ramona so that she couldn't return for her things? Ramona's plight was none of her business, she reminded herself. It was Tansy she needed to worry about. Guilt washed over her for not having found her sister yet. Catching her hair with Tansy's silver clasp so the lush length fell over one shoulder, she set out to meet her fate and maybe some answers in the Red Mesa Saloon.

Business was already picking up, and when Willow entered the saloon, at least a dozen heads turned in her direction. A buzz went around a table where a poker game was already in progress, Titus Whitiker being one of the players. Scattered around the room, customers and employees alike stared. A chill shot down Willow's spine. The way people were inspecting her...

She might have turned and run back up the stairs if Hazel hadn't popped out of the kitchen just then. The owner came straight toward Willow, giving her another once-over.

"You'll do, all right," Hazel said with satisfaction, her blue eyes aglow. "Ramona had nothing over you. Start circulating. Be friendly to customers. Encourage them to buy drinks."

"I can handle that," Willow said.

Still, as the night progressed, the odd feeling she'd started with grew. She was getting too much attention for her peace of mind. Some men stared outright. Others gave her covert looks even when the saloon's French songbird, Ottilie Robicheau, took the small stage to sing. The Nelson twins, Rosabelle and Amabelle, avoided her. And Benita Salgado, who would put on a flamenco display later, according to Hazel, didn't try to hide her animosity.

"Do not think you can take my place," Benita warned when they both collected drinks from the bartender.

"I'm not trying to take anything from anyone," Willow assured her.

But with a flash of her dark eyes, and a toss of her loose dark hair, Benita shouldered past her and carried drinks to the poker table, where every so often Titus stared out at *her*.

All the while, Willow did as Hazel had instructed. She talked with the customers and encouraged them to buy drinks. And whenever she found the opportunity, she asked about Tansy. Unfortunately, no flicker of recognition passed over any of the male faces when she described her sister.

Willow tried not to be discouraged—*someone* had to have seen Tansy.

Later, when the poker players took a break, the dealer came over to the end of the bar where Willow was waiting for her order to be filled. An attractive man, probably in his midthirties, he had sleek dark hair and a trim mustache. He'd removed his waistcoat; his shirtsleeves were fastened above the elbow with fancy embroidered garters that matched his vest.

"Farley Garnett," he said by way of introduction. "And you are?"

"Willow Kane."

"Damn, it's nearly like seeing a ghost!"

After the stir she'd caused, Willow shifted uneasily. "Whose ghost?"

"Ramona Cruz."

"Ramona is dead?"

Ramona . . . the woman whose job she had taken over . . . whose room she was using . . . whose skirt and blouse she was wearing?

"Murdered a coupla days ago."

Murdered.

That was even worse. The vigilantes had claimed Ryder Smith was a murderer. *Ramona's* murderer? she wondered with a start. And she'd set him free.

"No wonder people are staring—I'm wearing her things. Maybe I'd better get some new clothes."

"Wouldn't do much good unless you changed your looks, too," Farley informed her. "Even from a modest distance, you could pass for her—though up close, the differences are easier to see." He grinned. "You're a whole lot prettier, for one. As pretty as your name, Willow."

"And you're a flatterer."

"I only tell the truth."

Somehow, Willow got the feeling that Farley Garnett used the truth only when it suited him. "So what makes me look like Ramona?" she asked, wondering what he wanted from her.

"Coloring, mostly. Ramona had that same sun-kissed skin like you, not to mention black hair hanging over her shoulder and luminous light brown eyes."

"What about Benita? She's Mexican like Ramona was. I'm not." Though she owed what she looked like mostly to her half-breed father, her mother had been English and Irish rather than Spanish.

"It's the illusion you create. Benita doesn't carry herself as you do . . . as Ramona did . . . with a true and quiet confidence that comes from within."

"It's hard to be quiet in these," she joked, shaking her skirts to make the coins jingle.

On the other side of the bar, Hazel spoke up. "Ramona sewed small coins into the skirts of everything she wore. Said that way, she'd never be broke again."

Willow could empathize, considering her own money was no good in this century.

She was also certain it was wearing Ramona's things that added to the illusion of her being some kind of ghost, as Farley had commented. Trouble was, she couldn't afford to buy replacements. And why she was worrying about it, she couldn't say, Willow thought, other than wearing a dead woman's things being a tad morbid. Hopefully she'd find Tansy soon, maybe the very next day, and then they'd vanish back into their own time and she could forget everything that happened here.

Though Willow was uncertain she would ever forget Ryder Smith.

As fate would have it, the next time the saloon door opened, that very same man—the one she'd hoped never to see again—walked in as if he owned the place. Ryder was even better looking than she'd remembered. Certainly cleaner. The ruffles of his fancy white shirt seemed to gleam under the lamplight. More important, he appeared tougher, which, she realized, had something to do with his stance . . . as if he were challenging the room, daring someone, anyone, to stop him.

"Smith certainly has his nerve showing up here. Some think he did Ramona in," Farley muttered, heading back for the poker game.

And Willow's hands shook as she picked up the tray to deliver drinks to a far table. She could only hope that Ryder wouldn't recognize her, that he wouldn't stop to stare at her as had the other men in the room.

The same way he had the day before, Willow remembered. She'd thought his interest kind of spooky then. And now she knew why he'd been so fascinated. He'd been comparing her to Ramona.

A woman he'd been accused of murdering.

But had he?

The question plagued her as he walked over to the already busy poker table, obviously looking to enter the game. She served her drinks and collected money, including some paltry tips. Every penny would help, she supposed, but if room and board didn't come with the job, she'd be scavenging the street for a place to sleep.

Like Tansy might be.

The thought sobered Willow. She was standing at the bar, her mind spinning with images of her wild, passion-filled little sister, trying not to think the worst, when she felt a warm breath ruffle the back of her hair. She *knew* who was behind her before she glanced into the bar's mirror to confirm her assumption. *Ryder Smith.* Pulse in overdrive, she spun around, her gaze automatically going to his head.

"Can't see that lump you gave me unless you get closer," he said.

Refusing to apologize—he'd been keeping her from her search, Willow reminded herself—she said, "I obviously didn't stop you for long."

"Long enough."

Long enough for what? Willow's stomach was tying itself in a knot. Her mouth went dry. Ryder's stare was spooky, making her want to take a step in any direction . . . but toward him. She refused to let him intimidate her, however, so she compromised and stayed put.

"I got the impression you came here to gamble," she said caustically.

"Poker table's full. I need a distraction until someone folds and I can get in the game."

He was looking at her as if she fit the bill.

Willow glanced over to the table and saw that he was telling the truth about having to wait. Still, wanting to put that distance between them, she said, "If you'll excuse me, I have work to do," and tried to sweep right by him.

But Ryder caught her wrist and, once more, stopped her from getting away. He held her fast, though he didn't hurt her. Their gazes meshed and what she saw in his eyes made her suck in her breath. She knew that look. All male. On the hunt. What she didn't know was what exactly he wanted to do with her—a woman who'd not only saved his handsome hide, but who had bested him, as well.

A woman who looked enough like Ramona Cruz to make heads turn, including his.

"You can work at my table," Ryder told her. "Bring a bottle of tequila, lime, salt...and two glasses."

Willow would have liked to make some excuse, but Hazel was within hearing distance. The owner was already setting the requested items on a tray. And Ryder was grinning at her, obviously knowing she was trapped...and knowing she wasn't liking it one bit.

Chapter Four

Satisfaction that he'd won this hand warmed the cockles of Ryder's black gambler's heart. He had Miss Willow Kane exactly where he wanted her... for the moment, at least.

Squirming.

The dark beauty was definitely uncomfortable sitting next to him in a plush, velvet upholstered booth set back in a recessed alcove. All he had to do was reach out and pull a gold tasseled cord for the thick red drapes to drop in place. That would give them perfect privacy. And, oh, how he was tempted, if for no other reason than to enjoy Willow's reaction. She'd probably jump like a scared jackrabbit and hightail it out of the Red Mesa Saloon, if his fingers so much as reached for that silken tassel.

He contented himself that they sat painted by shadow, that after the initial stir he raised, some of the customers had gone back to their games of chance, while others were again paying rapt attention to the small stage where Benita Salgado superbly danced the flamenco, revealing flashes of bronzed limbs.

"Isn't that Miguel Borrego from the stable?" Willow asked, pointing at the guitar player accompanying Benita.

"He's been moonlighting here since I've been in Santa Fe."

"Then they're together?"

"Professionally. Borrego used to be personally involved with someone else . . . Ramona Cruz."

Ryder could sense Willow's immediate withdrawal and knew she'd learned the identity of the murdered woman. Not surprising, considering she was wearing Ramona's garments. Someone had been bound to tell her. Wondering what Hazel had been thinking of when she'd turned over Ramona's clothing to a woman who could pass for the dead saloon girl, he filled the two shot glasses before him to the brim.

"Drinking with the customers isn't part of my job," Willow protested.

Ryder raised a brow. "Hazel know that?"

She seemed undecided, but finally said, "All right."

Probably because she didn't want to sleep on the street that night. Ryder figured she wouldn't have taken this kind of work unless she was desperate. Not that a woman had much opportunity to work at anything else, unless her family was involved, he thought, remembering her talking about ranching. They had that in common, and the fact that neither of them was doing what they were born to . . .

"One drink," she added firmly. "But that's all."

"What?" Ryder snapped back to the present. "You not feeling well?"

"I'll be feeling too good after a shot of tequila. I need to work the night and I can't do that if I'm under the influence, now can I?"

Reflecting on the peculiar turn of phrase, Ryder sprinkled salt on his hand, over the flesh between the thumb and forefinger. He always took his tequila straight—after the salt and before the lime. Rather than licking the salt himself, though, he offered it to Willow.

"Ladies first," he said.

Ryder enjoyed the nervous reaction Willow tried to squelch and kept himself from laughing aloud only with grim determination.

"Unless you're afraid, of course."

He challenged her exactly as she had him about fixing up his neck, which still pained him. He hadn't gotten over the irony of her tending to his wound only to inflict another on him minutes later.

"And what should I be afraid of?"

"Yourself?" he asked, his voice still gravelly.

He shoved his hand closer, mesmerized by her tongue wetting her full lips. Then her warm mouth met his flesh, and she slowly sucked the salt from his hand, her luminous brown eyes watching for his reaction. Not about to give her any kind of satisfaction—that was *his* due, after all—Ryder gritted his teeth. He could only imagine what else that pretty mouth was capable of. Now *he* was shifting inside, his imagination growing by leaps and bounds, the proof of which strained against the material of his trousers.

Her mouth leaving his flesh was a relief, but Ryder couldn't look away as she downed the tequila. He watched the cords of her long neck work as the liquid burned down the inside of her throat.

She sorely tempted the devil in him. He could imagine running his tongue along her neck's length, savoring her slightly salty, slightly musky taste. He could imagine taking that mouth with his and drinking deep....

Eyes watering, Willow slapped down the shot glass. Ryder held out the wedge of lime, once more making her mouth come to his hand. At the brush of her lips against his flesh, sensations shot through him from the tips of his fingers straight to his groin.

Good Lord, he'd set out to sweetly torture Willow—her payment for the bump on his head—only he'd ended up torturing himself. What kind of damn fool was he? The kind who completed his own salt-tequila-lime ritual in a quarter of the time it had taken her. He concentrated on the liquid warmth coursing down through him to his gut.

When he tossed his lime onto the table, he realized Willow was gazing at him intently. And with some curiosity.

"What?"

"I was wondering why you'd show your face in a town where they wanted to hang you."

"The law's not after me." Though it should be, Ryder would give her that. "Only a few upstanding citizens decided to take the law into their own hands. From now on, I'll be more careful venturing into dark places." He couldn't help adding, "And I certainly won't turn my back on *you* again."

Willow had the grace to appear contrite. A becoming color stole up her neck and into her cheeks, and she was having trouble looking at him. Ryder wanted to take her chin in hand and force her to meet his gaze. But he was too involved here. He'd set out to play a simple game with the woman—to teach her a lesson—but to her credit, she'd somehow gotten the upper hand.

"It doesn't seem I did any permanent damage," Willow said primly.

"What?"

"To your head." She stared up at the general area where she'd clobbered him as if she'd like to take a closer look. "Does it hurt much?"

His turn to back off. "I'll survive." He wasn't about to let her get her hands on him...unless it was in a far more personal way.

"Sometimes we do things because we're desperate. I had to get away."

"That's right, I forced you to do it." That's what she'd said before his lights went out. "So you could rush into town to work in a saloon?"

"So I could try to find my sister."

Ryder remembered he'd meant to talk about that particular problem of hers over the supper they never shared. "You normally work as a rancher and can obviously take care of yourself. Why can't she?"

"Because Tansy's only fifteen."

Willow had a point. A girl that age could get herself into a heap of trouble without even trying. His sister had.

"So what made her run?"

"A stupid argument."

From the sudden tears springing to Willow's eyes, Ryder figured she felt guilty over that, too. "Did you check home?"

"I tried."

Whatever that meant. "But what makes you think she might have fled to Santa Fe?"

"Because she loves this town. And our mother lives here. Or will in the future," she muttered.

The last comment confused Ryder, until he remembered Willow insisting the year was 1995 rather than 1885. For a while there, he'd forgotten he was dealing with a pretty thing who happened to be a bit touched in the head.

He looked at her hard, trying to decide whether or not Willow seemed to be in her right mind now. At this moment, she appeared completely vulnerable, totally unlike the self-possessed woman who'd ridden to his rescue, the same woman who'd gotten the best of him. She blinked away the threat of tears and sniffed as if trying to regain control. Her full lower lip was quivering despite her obvious resolution. Some long-buried, protective instinct surfaced, and Ryder wanted more than anything to help Willow. But he didn't know how.

"Your turn," she said suddenly, looking out to the house.

He followed her gaze straight to the poker table, where a couple of cowpunchers were getting up, expressions grim. Probably lost their last month's pay.

"Well, aren't you going to get over there before someone else claims your seat?"

Ryder scowled at her. "How flattering that you want to get rid of me so badly."

"You're the one who wanted in on the poker game," she reminded him.

"True."

And if he was smart, he'd walk away from Miss Willow Kane and never look back. Let her handle her own troubles. Only he wasn't certain he wanted to walk away...until he spotted Cal Atchley heading for one of the table's empty seats. An opportunity too good to resist.

"If you'll excuse me." He lifted his hat from the upholstered seat and placed it on his head. "I have a varmint to skin. That's Cal Atchley, one of the wealthiest ranchers in the territory." He pulled some coins from a pocket, more than enough for the tequila and a generous tip, and threw them on the tray. "He's the one who set his boys on me."

But why?

Doubting Atchley's men had ridden straight for the Lazy A ranch without searching the countryside for him—they'd be afraid and embarrassed to admit their failure before expending all their resources to track him down again—Ryder figured the boss might not know about the miracle of his being rescued at the crucial moment.

Therefore, he couldn't wait to see the look on Cal Atchley's face when confronted with a supposedly hanged man demanding some answers.

WILLOW HAD NEVER experienced such a sense of relief as when Ryder Smith left her to her own devices. He'd been toying with her, and she guessed she deserved that. At least he hadn't taken out his revenge using violence, she thought, Ramona's death coming to mind. Had the late saloon girl done something to stir Ryder's animosity...or was that what the real murderer wanted everyone to think?

Ryder's interest had been sparked by the arrival of a middle-aged man with a comfortable paunch, silver-streaked brown hair, and a clean-shaven if jowly face. Judging by his well-tailored clothing, Cal Atchley probably could afford to lose more than a few double eagles—which she'd learned were twenty-dollar gold pieces. The last thing he looked like was a rancher, at least not any she knew. Not a speck of dust or a sign of hard work about him. She'd bet his hands were soft, too, his only calluses caused by shuffling cards.

How was Ryder so sure this Cal Atchley was responsible for the vigilantes that had almost ended his life?

Willow couldn't help herself. Sliding out of the booth, she placed the bottle and shot glasses on the tray and headed toward the poker table, her attention pinned to the drama about to be played out there.

Already sitting when Ryder stopped at the empty chair next to him, Atchley looked up, then turned white and gaped as if he were seeing a ghost. "Smith!" he choked out.

"Atchley. This seat taken?"

"N-no."

Ryder slid into the chair and pulled it closer to the other man. Willow could feel the tension sparking between them, as must the other poker players, who fell silent to watch the interchange.

"I feel as if we have some things to settle," Ryder was saying, "like why it is you set your boys on me."

Atchley shook his head in denial. "Don't know what you're talking about," he blustered.

"I think you do," Ryder insisted. "But what interest would you have in Ramona's death? Unless *you* were involved."

The rancher stiffened. "Why you good for nothing . . . you calling me a killer?"

"If the boot fits . . ."

Jowly face reddening, Atchley jumped up and lunged for Ryder, bunching his shirt at his throat and pulling him to his feet. Willow held her breath for Ryder's reaction. He merely gripped the other man's hand at the wrist until Atchley let go.

"That's better. Neck's still a bit sore from what your boys did to me."

"No account! Maligner!"

Atchley's hand dropped—obviously going for his weapon—but even as his fingers brushed his holster, a gun appeared in Ryder's hand quicker than Willow could swallow. Now the entire room went dead silent.

"As you can see," Ryder said quietly, "that wasn't smart. But then you're not a real smart man or you would've seen to my death yourself. Now you'll never know what's waiting for you around the corner."

"Put that gun away!" Hazel shouted from behind the bar. "I don't want no trouble in here. You take your quarrel out to the street and now!"

"I'm not shooting anyone...tonight," Ryder said, holstering his weapon. Without taking his eyes off Atchley, he nodded to the poker dealer. "Don't bother cutting me in, Farley. Changed my mind. Can't stand the rank odor at this table. Some fresh air'll do me good."

With that, he backed off to the door and disappeared into the night.

And the room lit with repressed energy, filled with excited voices and speculation. Willow moved toward the bar. Trembling inside, she realized Ryder Smith was dangerous. And he had a special interest in her. She hadn't missed the extra money he'd thrown on her tray, the best tip she'd had all night.

"Is this place always so lively?" she asked Hazel.

"Boys gotta let off steam once in a while. Usually I convince 'em to take their arguments elsewhere. Sometimes with a little help," the owner added, lifting the shotgun she'd been holding out of sight behind the counter so Willow could see it.

"Thank God you didn't have to use that," Willow said, shuddering.

"Ryder's normally a reasonable man."

Normally? Willow wondered what that meant. Hazel didn't say, though, merely replaced the shotgun on its rack under the bar and went to take care of a new customer at the other end.

"Good thing Atchley didn't press him," Benita said, sidling up to the bar with empties.

"You don't think Ryder would have killed him?" Willow asked, hoping not.

Benita stared at her. "You don't know much about real men, do you?"

"The real men I know aren't prone to violence."

Though she had to admit she lived in a different century. And it wasn't like she knew many men other than her wranglers and some neighboring ranchers. Taking care of Rancho Milagro and Grandpa Jonah and Tansy took up all of her time. She rarely had any energy left to socialize. She read enough, though, to know violence was on the rise in the more crowded cities.

"Where'd you say you were from?" Benita asked.

"New Mexico Territory, but a good piece from here," Willow hedged.

"So is Ryder Smith...aways east from here, that is. No one knows exactly how far."

"So he's a man of mystery?"

Benita seemed to be enjoying herself. "Ryder's a professional gambler. He rode into Santa Fe nearly a year ago, but never said where from. He doesn't talk about his past. But from the way he carries himself...the way he handles that Colt .45 of his...rumor is he has more than one person's blood on his hands."

Shocked, Willow realized Benita was intimating Ryder had been a professional gunfighter. He himself had scared her into believing it. Then, again, she'd sensed he was full of as much bluff as danger, a quality more suited to the professional gambler he now claimed to be. He might have made her pulse pound out of control, might have embarrassed her, but he hadn't hurt her any.

"If he *was* a gunfighter, what's he doing making his living with a deck of cards?"

"Maybe the law's after him," Benita speculated. "Could be he's laying low."

"Have you seen any Wanted posters for him?"

"For Ryder *Smith?*" Benita asked. "No."

Her purposeful emphasis left Willow to wonder if Smith was, indeed, Ryder's real last name. Then Willow told herself to consider the source. Benita could be unpleasant, as she'd experienced for herself. Moreover, she seemed to delight in spreading dirt on a man who wasn't around to defend himself. Even if Smith was a common name that shady people took to hide their true identities, who was to say it wasn't Ryder's true last name?

Nothing untoward happened the rest of the night, and Benita went back to treating Willow as some kind of rival. Just as well. Benita wasn't the sort of person Willow cared to embrace as a friend anyway.

Serving drinks and keeping customers company for a while, she had plenty of opportunity to ask after Tansy. Time and again, however, she got the same depressing answer. No one admitted to having seen a young girl with bright red hair in the past few days.

And with each negative response, Willow's worry grew. She was relieved when the clientele began drifting off shortly after midnight and Hazel gave her the sign that she could leave. Not that she planned on immediately going upstairs to the inviting bed that awaited her. The thought that Tansy might not have a comfortable place to stay, that she might be sleeping in some back alley, tortured her. If she didn't get out there and look for her sister until she was blind with exhaustion, she feared she wouldn't be able to sleep at all.

The night air was cooler than she'd expected, but Willow used that to keep herself moving fast. Going east and then south, she tore down the narrow streets of Santa Fe, encountering only a few men whose invitations she ignored.

She poked her head in every courtyard and alley she passed, hoping and yet afraid to find her sister huddled and petrified in some dank corner. She crossed the Santa Fe River and soon found herself on El Camino de Cañon, better known to her and thousands of twentieth-century people as Canyon Road.

By the light of a waning moon, Willow gazed out at the mountains hulking against the night sky ahead. Her feet like lead, her head muzzy with exhaustion, she started down the dark, winding road lined with adobe buildings, nearly all residences with enclosed courtyards. She couldn't imagine Tansy taking refuge in this part of town, even though her sister did love window shopping here in their own time. A century hence, most of these private residences would be turned into art galleries and clothing boutiques and trendy restaurants.

But at this time in its development, the neighborhood was not one a teenager could easily lose herself in. As Willow checked the grounds of one home, a vigilant dog barked a warning to its owner.

Choosing to give up for the night rather than explain her presence in a private courtyard, Willow turned out onto the street and was startled by an abrupt movement ahead blending with the shadows. She hesitated. Was someone truly there or was she so tired her imagination was tricking her?

Mouth dry, she moved down the road, then hugged a building surrounded by juniper bushes and ponderosa pines and patiently waited. A moment later, the shadow up the street separated into two. Her heart pounded ... surely not Tansy ... but no, the silhouette was too large to be her sister's. Besides, there was something furtive, something sinister about the person's movements, and gut instinct told Willow that same someone was following her. Even as the silhouette blended with another shadow and seemed to melt into the night, her stomach knotted with tension.

Backing off, a jingling reminded Willow of the coins sewn into her petticoats. The slight tinkling noise carried along the otherwise silent street, undoubtedly straight to her stalker. She gathered her skirts close to her chest in a vain attempt to sneak off unheard, for no matter how carefully she crept, some coins she couldn't contain threatened to give her away.

Hoping to lose whoever was pursuing her, she ducked into an unlocked courtyard and waited, pressed up against the trunk of an aspen tree for what seemed like forever. Her heart thumped against her ribs; her nerves skittered as she waited. She neither saw nor heard anyone pass by. An errant breeze shook the aspen's leaves. The rustling sound shivered up her spine and pushed her back onto Canyon Road.

Her gaze piercing the dark around her, Willow saw nothing ... and yet she sensed the other presence, malevolent and angry, nearby.

What to do?

The nature of the old streets presented a problem. Willow was on the opposite side of the river from where she wanted to be. And whoever was following her stood between her and the bridge that was part of the Paseo de Peralta, the road that circled the heart of town. But what alternative did she have? Willow thought a minute before choosing to follow the riverbed rather than backtracking the way she'd come.

Only a few streets cut across Canyon Road, however, and so she swept farther east, paralleling the river, getting even farther from the bridge that would take her back toward the Red Mesa Saloon, until she finally came to a narrow turnoff. Then she dropped her skirts and ran like the devil was on her heels— which he might be for all she knew—her boots pummeling the dirt street, Ramona's coins jingling like mad.

When she reached the little-used, rutted road that ran behind the houses, she backtracked toward the bridge, moving ever closer to the river and the cover it offered. Eventually, the road ended altogether, and she found herself in the shelter of cottonwoods and junipers, fighting the shorter wild growth of gama and buffalo grasses that spurted around her, flowing upward from the riverbank.

From some distance behind, she heard the quick pad of feet slapping against the dirt road. She ducked down, determined not to give away her hiding place.

The break couldn't have come at a better time, for she'd been traveling at such a pace she could hardly breathe, and her heart felt ready to thump through the wall of her chest. She concentrated, centered herself, quieted her pulse and lungs.

Meanwhile, her stalker swept to the end of the road and continued the race through the brush. Willow strained to see through the plant life hiding her, but the silhouette was indistinguishable, gave her no clue whatsoever as to her pursuer's identity.

Again she waited, patient, listening hard. Eventually she heard the slap of leather against wood—boots against bridge. Her pursuer was heading back toward town.

As would Willow, once convinced she was safe.

Some time passed, maybe a half hour or so. Willow sneaked from her hiding place, alert to any other presence, any hidden danger as she approached the bridge. Nothing. Probably some drunken amorous cowboy had been pursuing her, and once he realized his quest was fruitless, he'd given up and had gone somewhere to sleep it off.

At least that's what she preferred to think, especially considering her other options, like one of the vigilantes.

Relieved, Willow quickly crossed the river, taking the Paseo around to the east side of town, never once letting down her guard.

Not until she entered the courtyard leading to the Red Mesa Saloon and the rooms above it. Her temporary home.

Only then did Willow feel another presence . . . one directly behind her. She whirled around and found herself flattened against a ruffled chest.

As she jumped back, a familiar, taunting voice asked, "Walking the streets?"

Heart thumping as much from his very nearness as from an accretion of fright, Willow stared up into the half-shadowed face of Ryder Smith. Lit lamps in the courtyard allowed her to recognize the man. "Where did you come from?"

"What does it matter?"

Then the obvious struck her. "Have you been following me?" she asked indignantly.

"Guilty conscience?"

Ready to spit nails, Willow told herself to calm down. Ryder was teasing her. He wouldn't be trying to have fun with her if he'd been the one trying to frighten her only a short time ago. Right?

"Guilty about what?" she asked. "Saving your hide?"

But his suddenly strident, "What the hell kind of a game are you playing with me, Willow Kane?" made her go all tense inside again.

"I'm not playing any games."

"Saving me from a hanging...leaving me unconscious...then next time I see you it's at my place of business...and you're wearing *her* clothes, looking too much like her for anyone's comfort."

"Ramona's." Willow had been through too much in the last hour to cower now. Besides, she was in the middle of town. A scream would bring people running. She hoped. She went on the offensive. "Why do people around here think you killed Ramona Cruz, anyway?"

His silent stare sent shivers down her spine. Then, reluctantly, he said, "I have a stack of my own special chips I keep on the table for luck when I play poker. Don't actually use 'em anymore. And those chips don't leave the casino except with me. And Ramona . . . just that once . . . Them that found her body pried one out of her closed fist."

Willow frowned and tried to remember some cop shows she'd seen on television lately. Would the fact that the dead woman had something that belonged to Ryder constitute enough physical evidence to make him a suspect?

Maybe.

"So, what do you say?" he was asking her. "Who put you up to this charade?"

Snapped back into the present, Willow insisted, "No one put me up to anything. My ending up at the Red Mesa was a coincidence, is all." She tried to keep her voice steady. "Hazel had an open job she needed filled. She also had a spare room and spare clothes. She wanted me dressed in something more feminine than pants and a vest."

"The outfit does suit you better."

She ignored the quick shift in tone, the semblance of a compliment. "So is that why you've been following me? Trying scare tactics?"

His turn to frown. "I might have tried to scare you, but I wasn't following you."

Willow didn't know whether to believe Ryder or not. She kept experiencing a healthy dose of fear around this man . . . but the fear now tasted different than what she'd endured earlier, possibly running for her very life. This was far more subtle—and somehow more threatening to her inner well-being.

"It's late."

She swung around, intending to go straight to her room.

Ryder's hand fastening on to her arm stopped her. She felt the imprint of each finger on her flesh. Warmth that had nothing to do with fear flushed through her, and she suddenly felt bandy-legged.

Damn!

"Whatever the truth of the matter," Ryder began in a low, husky voice that thrilled her, "you oughta know you look too much like a dead woman for a killer's comfort."

The implied threat banished any warmth Willow might be feeling toward Ryder.

Swallowing hard, she freed herself and escaped up the back stairs and to her room. After slamming the door and locking it, she dragged out her rifle from under her bed, checking to make certain the weapon was loaded.

After which she stripped off the dead woman's clothes—Willow only wished she could burn the damned things, but then she'd have nothing to wear on the job. She pulled on her own pants, shirt and vest, then she hunkered down on the still-made bed, her rifle next to her.

She was ready.

Just in case...

RAMONA CRUZ was supposed to be dead. The knife had done its job, slicing easily into her lush body. Her blood had poured from the wound. So much blood. All over her clothing. All over the ground.

She had to be dead.

So what was she doing haunting the streets of Santa Fe?

A ghost.

The thought was enough to make anyone sweat inside. Already haunted by the past... wasn't one ghost enough?

Did ghosts appear in daylight? His didn't, but hers did. She didn't seem to have any rules. A ghost was supposed to have rules about when it could and could not appear, about what it could do, where it could go.

A ghost without rules... was it possible? asked a detached voice.

Or was it possible that she wasn't a ghost at all?

Maybe Ramona Cruz wasn't dead. Maybe the blood hadn't been so plentiful, merely startling in its intense red flow. Maybe the wound had been too shallow—the knife having missed any vital organs—to do much damage.

The thought that Ramona could be alive, that she could be flesh and blood, felt a bit better. For fixing a ghost would be next to near impossible.

But wringing the life out of a woman who didn't want to stay dead...

That could be arranged.

Chapter Five

"You again? You're not welcome here!" Titus Whitiker shouted, spittle spraying from his lips. "I didn't figure you for a stupid woman!"

A wide-eyed Willow stared at the shopkeeper, who was definitely out of control. "I came to buy a few things," she said. She'd made enough in tips to buy a bar of soap and something to sweeten her breath. Not to mention that she'd planned on checking back with Velma as she'd said she would.

A red-faced Titus was saying, "We don't need your kind—"

When Velma interrupted with a sweet-sounding, yet firm, "Titus, dear," as she entered from a back room. "Miss Kane is a customer. We *need* customers to stay in business, remember?"

"Yes, but—"

"Why don't you go on in the back and finish the inventory of the stock," Velma said in that same voice. "We discussed this last night, remember?"

To Willow's amazement, Titus seemed to grow docile before her very eyes. His shoulders rounded and his head nodded in agreement.

"If you're certain," he said, running a hand through his hair and shaking his head as if he'd just awakened from a nightmare.

"I am certain, dear. Now run along."

He trotted off, not unlike a pet lapdog. Willow stifled an ironic smile by biting the inside of her lip.

Velma fluttered around her. "Dear, dear, how I regret my husband's rudeness."

Willow felt sorry for the woman. "If he thinks Ryder Smith is a murderer, I guess he has reason to be angry with me."

Though why, she couldn't say. What was Ramona Cruz to Titus Whitiker that he would want vengeance for her death?

"I need a few personal items," she told Velma, who got them for her and rang up the sale.

"We never had our tea yesterday," the shopkeeper murmured. "Perhaps now?"

"I wish I could." Willow stuck her things in a deep vest pocket. "But I'm still looking for my sister. I wanted to check back, see if Tansy came in here."

Velma shook her head. "I know how I felt when my boy up and ran away. I'm so sorry."

Not nearly as sorry as Willow. She'd been out looking for Tansy since she'd awakened, her efforts to no avail. She'd checked businesses of every sort. In the midst of it all, the thought came to her that maybe Tansy hadn't come to Santa Fe as she'd assumed, that maybe she ought to return to the pueblo ruins and check again for further signs of her sister.

A tinkling warned Willow that another customer was entering. She glanced at the door and stiffened when she recognized the tall, broadly built man with shoulder-length black hair. The man she'd seen in the old house on Rancho Milagro property. The original owner? Could he be an ancestor? He was obviously some combination of Anglo and Hispanic and Indian. As far as she knew, however, there'd been no mixed blood in her family tree until her mother met her father.

Velma smiled up tremulously at the dark-visaged man. "What can I do for you today, Mr. Madrid?"

"Madrid?" Willow echoed, staring.

He turned his black eyes on her. "Wolf Madrid. What's it to you?"

That he was so mean looking when he challenged her made Willow back up a step. "I seem to have heard the name before, that's all."

"You've probably heard of Mr. Madrid because he's the best bounty hunter around," Velma said.

Actually, Wolf Madrid, Bounty Hunter, was the star of those dime novels Tansy read . . . ones written by a Kane ancestor! So he was as real as Buffalo Bill, Willow mused.

But, "Probably," was all she replied.

"You got someone you want me to round up for you?"

"What?"

"The way you're staring. Normally people only stare like that if they want me to work for 'em . . . or if they're shocked." He glared in return, his black gaze roaming over her face and hair. "But you ain't got much to be shocked at, now do you?"

Another reference to her mixed heritage. Willow didn't take offense, however, not considering the source. Besides, she had been staring rudely.

But before she could offer an apology, Madrid said, "Unless there's some *other* reason you're interested."

Not missing the implication, Willow narrowed her gaze and stood straighter. "I'll be going now. Velma, thanks for your hospitality. I'll probably be back tomorrow."

"See you then."

It was only after she'd left the store that it occurred to Willow that Madrid could help her. He was a bounty hunter, after all. He should be able to find one fifteen-year-old redhead. *Bounty* was the sticky part. She had none to offer, at least not in this century. She supposed she could tell Mr. Wolf Madrid all he had to do was follow her into the future to collect his reward, but then he would either laugh himself silly...or have her committed.

She approached the stable where Miguel Borrego was taking a *siesta* in one of the stalls. Her moving around, saddling Tequila, awoke him, however.

Yawning, he stood and watched her tighten the cinch. His eyes were spooky on her, like before, and she remembered Ryder telling her that Borrego had been personally involved with Ramona Cruz.

"Not leaving town with bills to pay, are you, Señorita Kane?" he asked with another yawn.

"I'll be back. I have a job at the saloon, remember?"

He looked her gear over, obviously noting she hadn't dragged her saddlebags or rifle along, and nodded. "I trust you." Though his eyes said differently.

"Good."

Willow felt that weird gaze follow her out of the stable, and thought twice about going back to her room to get her rifle. She didn't want to put a lie to her words. She wouldn't need the rifle anyway, she reasoned. How often could one person interrupt vigilantes at work?

Besides, she was armed. Her knife was cradled in the sheath at her belt, Willow thought, comforted.

Leaving the stable, she noticed Benita Salgado coming straight for it. To see Miguel?

With a friendly wave that wasn't returned, trying not to let Benita's snooty attitude get to her, Willow headed straight out of town the way she'd come. Then, passing the Whitiker General Store, she couldn't miss Wolf Madrid, shoulder shoved against the plate-glass window as if he'd been waiting for her to ride by. And on the other side, Titus and Velma were in the midst of a heated argument, though they stopped and stared when they caught sight of her.

Madrid's black eyes followed her, and a shiver coursed through her. She was hard-pressed to shake away the macabre sensation of meeting in person someone she'd assumed was a fictional legend. He appeared every bit as hard and mean as he'd been portrayed by the artist, she'd give him that.

An eerie feeling stayed with her straight into open country. Once when she glanced over her shoulder, Willow swore she saw the dust of another rider in the distance. Of course, that didn't mean the rider was after her, just that she wasn't alone in God's country. Nothing sinister in that.

Shrugging the matter off as coincidence, she went on her way, only at a faster pace.

After riding Tequila as hard as she dared all the way back to the pueblo ruins, Willow dismounted and tied the reins to one of the cottonwoods. Then she stooped down to a narrow stream and refreshed herself, sipping at water and letting more trickle over her face and neck. While it was only May, the sun was warm enough, that was for certain. The gelding whinnied for her attention.

"Sorry, boy," she told him. "You'll have to wait a while till you cool some." She'd water him before starting back to town.

Meanwhile, she went over the soft ground around the area where the ribbon of water pooled. The prints she'd seen before were less evident—the wind had eroded them some—but still there. No unusual brand-type markings other than those made by Tequila. She studied the two sets of boot prints and again came to the conclusion that two people of very different stature had ridden out together.

The smaller of the two probably had been Tansy. So where had they ridden?

The same physical evidence, and yet she had new information she hadn't had the last time, Willow mused. She now knew she was in the nineteenth century rather than the twentieth, as was Tansy.

No doubt Madrid—her sister's horse, not the bounty hunter—had been left back in the twentieth century. Willow tried not to worry that he needed to be watered and fed. Surely Grandpa Jonah had the sheriff's department out there and they'd found the poor beast. She wondered what they would think had happened to *her*. Not that she had room to worry about one more thing.

Back to the past, where she was stuck.

Madrid hadn't been with Tansy up at the kiva as Tequila had been with her. That meant when her sister had made the leap in time, she would have been on foot, not knowing about the time shift. Probably figuring Madrid had somehow gotten himself loose and had headed for home. And probably a stranger watering his own horse at the stream had offered Tansy the equivalent of a twentieth-century lift home.

Only home didn't exist, as Willow had learned the hard way. Then what? What would a fifteen-year-old do if not go into Santa Fe, at least a familiar place that she could relate to? Come back here to find her way home?

Could Tansy have gone up to the pueblo ruins and figured out how to get herself back to her own time?

Speculating as she went, Willow climbed up the incline and concentrated on looking for other new footprints. None on the main path. That is, no boot prints. She was certain someone wearing moccasins had been up here, but they were man-size, not fifteen-year-old-girl-size. And she didn't have to worry about being surprised by the wearer, for the prints went both ways. The man had come and gone.

What was left of Tequila's hoofprints and her own boot prints—and Tansy's—only went one way.

Down.

Still, while this was the easy way, it wasn't the only path up to the ruins.

And to her surprise, Willow realized the old pueblo wasn't quite as *ruined* as she'd remembered it. That made sense, considering what was left of the buildings had another one hundred and ten years to crumble under the stress of the elements before catching up with her present. More of the walls were intact. And some of the archways. And she could see a crude staircase of footholds cut into the rock face of the mesa itself. By the twentieth century, they had eroded to the point that she hadn't known they existed.

But Willow imagined an adventurous fifteen-year-old might prefer scrambling and climbing her way up, so Tansy might have made her way back to the kiva using them.

Wishful thinking.

For when she reached the kiva area once more, she saw no new prints left by boots. Tansy had not returned. As far as Willow knew, her sister hadn't been to Santa Fe, either. Then where in blue blazes had she gone?

As if to echo that thought, Tequila snorted and whinnied below.

"I won't be long, boy!" she shouted, hoping the sound of her voice would settle him down.

Elbows wedged on the now-solid ledge surrounding the opening to the lower chamber of the kiva, Willow went over the clues she'd found the day she started her pursuit. Like the single horse tracks. As far as she could tell, those tracks had led straight for the old ranch house. That gave her pause. Could the man who'd offered her sister a ride be none other than Wolf Madrid, Tansy's dime-novel hero, himself? Having had too close an encounter with the man for her peace of mind, Willow went cold inside.

Especially when she considered her sister might have been in the house while she hid out behind the junipers!

Heart pounding, Willow vowed to check out the old ranch house when she left. But she was all alone, against a bounty hunter fierce enough to make most men quake in their boots. Then she'd face down Wolf Madrid with a loaded rifle. And if he had Tansy...

Suddenly realizing her rifle was back under her bed, Willow trashed that plan. She couldn't face the bounty hunter with nothing but a knife, that was for certain. A vague noise like rock being kicked caught her attention—no doubt Tequila getting restless. She'd have to get back to him, just as she'd have to think of something else.

Then Willow warned herself that she shouldn't be reaching, shouldn't let her imagination run along the lines of those dime novels that held Tansy enthralled.

The horse carrying two people could have belonged to anyone, for heaven's sake. Besides, she hadn't followed the tracks all the way to their destination, since she'd been waylaid by a bunch of vigilantes and one very confusing gambler.

If that's what Ryder Smith was, Willow mused, remembering Benita intimating that he might have been a gunfighter in a former life. Benita didn't like her and could have been lying. How could she tell? How could she know the truth when she saw it? Stuck in a time warp, Willow was getting the idea that nothing was exactly as it seemed. About to get Tequila and ride back to Santa Fe, Willow jumped when a noise came from directly behind her.

Even as she started to turn, she felt the threat . . .

. . . and the hard hands shoving into her back.

Willow tried to catch herself, but it was too late. She flipped forward, headfirst, flying into the kiva's lower chamber.

THE FIRST THING she recognized was that she had a royal headache the size of the Grand Canyon. The second was that someone was calling her name.

"Willow!" came the renewed shout.

She blinked her eyes open and tried to adjust, but she could see little in the dark cavern where she'd fallen. She focused on the hole above where daylight still shone.

"Willow!" The voice was closer. Male. And familiar.

Heart thumping, she forced herself into a sitting position. Her head whirled. Uncertain if she was thinking clearly, she yelled back.

"Ryder, I'm here!"

"Where?"

"The kiva." She only hoped he knew what that was.

Willow was still trying to get her bearings when she heard a boot scuffle directly overhead. Looking up too quickly, she winced and clenched her jaw.

What was the nineteenth-century equivalent of extra-strength aspirin, anyway?

"How the hell did you get yourself down there?" Ryder demanded.

She glared up at his silhouette. "I thought jumping down here would be an amusing way to pass the time."

"I could leave you here." He started to pull away.

"No!" she said in a breathless panic, knowing she couldn't get herself out. "Please."

But he was already leaning over the entryway, undoubtedly trying to get a good look at the situation. "That's better. Nothing's broken?"

"Just my head. I must have hit it when I fell." Hard. Willow searched for the wound until her fingers found the scraped lump. She winced. "You going to keep asking me questions or get me out of here?"

Pueblo Indians had used ladders to climb down into the sacred chamber. She doubted she'd find one of those lying around, waiting for her.

"Gotta leave you alone for a few minutes," Ryder said, his tone a reassuring one. "Didn't think to carry a rope with me." The silhouette pulled away from the opening for a second before popping back in place. "Don't let yourself fall asleep, Willow. Don't even close your eyes."

"I won't."

So Ryder knew something about concussions. She hoped that would make him hurry. She wasn't fond of dank, dark places without easy exit. Who knew what might be keeping her company in the cavern?

Who knew what would have happened to her had Ryder not showed?

Furthermore, why had he?

Not wanting to think about anything too deep with her head thumping like the inside of a bass drum, Willow tried concentrating instead on rising to her feet. Her world spun and she sank back down to the ground for a moment. She took a deep breath, let it out slowly and tried again, this time gathering herself onto her knees first. From the kneeling position, she shoved upward. Her surroundings rocked just a little before settling back in place.

Only when she was on her feet did she wonder how long she might have to stay upright without support. She wanted to sink back to the damp floor, wanted to close her eyes again in the worst way....

Until quick steps above warned her of Ryder's approach. She took a deep, steadying breath.

"You still awake?"

"My eyes are open." The best she could say for her state of mind. "And I'm on my feet."

"Good." He threw down some rope. "Put this over your head and around your waist."

The rope was already looped, reminding her of the hangman's noose she'd saved Ryder from. Which reminded her of meeting that same hangman in the Whitiker General Store. She suppressed a shudder. *This* rope was going to get her out of trouble rather than cause more for her. Taking the line in hand, she wondered if it might not cut her in half when the loop tightened around her middle.

"Maybe I'd better just put my foot in the loop," she suggested. "I can hold on and stand while you pull me up."

"And what if you have trouble hanging on and flip over on your head?"

He had a point. "Are you always right?" Willow grumbled, slipping the rope in place around her middle. "What are you going to anchor me to up there, anyhow? I don't think much of the ruins is too stable."

"*I'm* stable enough," Ryder said. "I've got this end around me, and when you say the word, I'll start backing away from the opening."

"I'm ready."

His slow, steady gait stretched her upward so she was on tiptoe one minute, dangling in the air the next. The rope tightened around her middle just as she had feared, making it difficult for her to breathe normally, which in turn brought back the wooziness. Though she clung to the line above her with both hands, Willow disobeyed Ryder and for the tiniest moment closed her eyes to make everything stop spinning.

If she didn't get herself under control—and quick— she was bound to be sick.

Not an attractive picture.

The rope's inching stopped for a moment. "Hey, how you doing down there?" Ryder called.

"Not as far down as I was," she joked, biting back a groan when her stomach did a little dance. "So, that's pretty good, I guess. Keep going." A moment later and several inches higher, Willow was able to reach out and grab hold of rock. "I'm just about there."

Ryder gave her another boost. Placing her other hand over the lip of the kiva opening, Willow clung to the stone tenaciously. The next thing she knew, Ryder was there. He reached over, grabbed her by the seat of her pants and lifted enough of her weight that she was able to scramble up and into his arms.

Willow wrapped both arms around his neck. Ryder backed up, pulling her completely free of the opening. The rope was wrapped a number of times around his waist. Filled with relief and gratitude, she sagged against the scratchy bulk, not to mention the warmth of his chest—for once the fancy man wasn't wearing a ruffled shirt.

Again, her world was spinning, but this time Willow wasn't certain the sensation was due totally to the head injury. For some inexplicable reason, Ryder had this strange effect on her...just as she seemed to have on him, if his expression was any indication. He was staring at her with a mixture of concern and intensity that made her grow warm all over.

Before she knew what he was about, he ducked his head forward, his mouth crashing into hers, devouring her as if he were a starving man.

Surprised, strangely elated, Willow offered herself to Ryder as a tasty treat, kissing him back with as much enthusiasm as she could muster to obliterate the circumstances.

But underneath her fright and thankfulness, something deeper stirred inside her. The same something that had attracted her to him from the first. Willow tightened her arms around his neck, and he pressed her closer to him. Her stomach crammed against the lengths of rope he'd wrapped around himself, but her breasts met his chest in a sensual motion that made the tender flesh pebble.

"Oh, my." Willow sighed when he abruptly ended the kiss.

Unwinding her arms from his neck, still bruised but healing, she trailed one hand along Ryder's cheek, the pads of her fingers lingering on his thick mustache, so much darker than the molten gold that haloed his too-handsome Robert Redford-Sundance Kid face. Fascinating. She'd never kissed a man with a mustache before. Hadn't plain been kissed by any man in far too long to admit... if she could even remember when exactly.

A sad commentary on her life, Willow thought. All work, no play. If only she had someone with whom she could share the responsibilities....

When Ryder nipped her callused fingertip, the zinging along her nerve endings made her quickly withdraw her hand. Suddenly in the throes of as much confusion as attraction, Willow had the distinct impression that Ryder was equally wary of her.

"Can you walk?"

"Of course I can walk."

Her insistence came too soon. For the moment she took a step away from him, her knees wobbled and threatened to heave her back to the ground. No chance, though, for Ryder wrapped a steadying arm around her back, and as quickly as he'd kissed her a moment ago, swung her up into his arms.

No use in fighting, Willow told herself. She didn't have the energy—not to mention her distinct lack of desire to get away from him anytime soon. With a sigh, she rested her head on Ryder's shoulder and thrilled at the sensation of his heart beating strong and fast against the side of her breast. For a moment, she imagined what it would be like to do more than kiss the man.

Her hero.

Feeling like a dime-novel heroine—she'd *never* been carried around before!—Willow suppressed a euphoric giggle lest Ryder think she was mocking him. The instinct to laugh reflected her relief at being free of the cavern while entangled in this unusual situation. At Rancho Milagro, she was in charge of any number of men. Somehow, Ryder Smith had managed to put himself in charge of her.

Willow was actually regretful when they arrived back at the stream and Ryder set her down. Her feet touched solid ground, the physical connection joltingly broken. And yet, as Ryder attended to removing the rope from her waist, the way his hands worked along her flesh...

Heart pounding, aware of heat creeping up her neck as well as in most other directions, Willow glanced away while he finished. Her gaze took in the stream, rocks, cottonwoods. A moment passed before she registered that Tequila was missing. Then she remembered how the horse had neighed restlessly earlier, as if someone else was there.

Someone *had* been there.

The someone who'd pushed her into the lower chamber of the kiva, Willow realized with a shudder. How peculiar that Ryder knew where to find her.

Not to mention his knowing that she needed finding, at all!

Chapter Six

Willow thought about it. She'd run into Ryder the night before, too, after she'd been followed along Canyon Road. Of course she'd tried putting off that incident to some drunken amorous cowboy, but deep down she knew she'd made enemies when she'd rescued Ryder.

Filled with curiosity—she'd rather call it curiosity than suspicion—Willow stared at Ryder as he unwound the rope from his own waist.

Her voice was even when she asked, "How did you know to look for me?"

His brilliant blue eyes were candid. "Your horse."

"Tequila told you I was in trouble?"

Ryder nodded, wound the rope into a loose coil and fastened it to his saddle. "So to speak. I saw Borrego stabling him, but he was all lathered up. I asked what you'd been up to, riding him that way. Borrego said he didn't know what happened, that Tequila came back to town riderless."

"So you figured something was wrong," she said, frowning at the pain in her head.

As if realizing that, he calmly ordered, "Sit down here a minute," and gently moved Willow onto a small

boulder. Removing his bandanna, he wet it in the
stream. Then he poked through her hair around the
site of her injury and placed the cold, wet cloth carefully on the sore spot. She winced at the fresh pain,
though she knew the cold might help a bit.

"I figured you must have been thrown and were
hiking back to Santa Fe on foot," Ryder said.

Whoever had pushed her had released Tequila and
had sent him galloping in the right direction. Odd that
the horse would have gone all the way back into Santa
Fe... unless maybe he was led off in that direction by
her attacker, of course.

Scalp starting to feel a bit numb from the cold,
Willow could hardly wait until Ryder was finished
with her. When he removed the bandanna, he checked
her eyes.

"So you decided to come find me and give me a lift
back into town, huh?" she asked, rising.

Ryder's gaze was narrowed on her, no doubt because she'd used a twentieth-century term. "Lucky
your horse has those fancy shoes. I was able to pick up
his tracks a ways out of Santa Fe. I never figured I'd
have to track you all the way out here."

Which sounded plausible enough, Willow told herself. Besides, she had no reason to disbelieve him, to
think Ryder'd have some reason to want to hurt her.
After all, she had saved his life....

Startled by the thought that followed, she said,
"Looks like we're even Steven."

She stooped to check out the ground around the
watering hole. Fresh hoofprints. Ones other than Tequila's. Nothing unusual about them—except that one
of the prints was smeared and a bit off-kilter, as if the
horse's rear right shoe was working loose.

Again he gave her the odd look. "We're what?"

"Even Steven. I saved your skin, now you saved mine. So that evens things out, right?"

"I guess," Ryder agreed, his expression darkening. "One thing, though, what the hell were you doing out here alone in the first place?"

As if she had to answer to him or anyone else for her actions. Willow drew herself up to her full height, though she was still several inches shorter than Ryder.

"Looking for my sister." Whom she'd managed to forget yet again. She hadn't given Tansy one thought since Ryder came to her rescue. He did know how to distract a woman. "Your horse have a shoe loose?"

"No." Following her lead, he changed the subject right back. "You were searching for your sister out here, rather than at home, wherever that might be?"

Willow thought to explain again. Certain he hadn't forgotten her insisting the year was 1995, however, she suspected Ryder already questioned her sanity. Maybe that's why he'd come for her. Figured she didn't need to be wandering out in the sun too long. Might have forgotten her hat.

She had forgotten her hat down in the kiva, she realized. Sighing, she said, "Never mind."

"You'd better learn to be more careful if you don't want to end up as feed for the buzzards."

"I'm always careful." Some things a person just couldn't predict.

"That's why you fell into a hole that you couldn't get out of."

"I didn't fall. I was pushed."

"What?"

"You know, someone came up behind me and *pow!*" She demonstrated.

He seemed genuinely surprised—and disturbed. "Who?" He was looking at her with that same expression he'd had when she'd argued with him about the year.

"Someone whose horse had a loose shoe." Not liking his suddenly thunderous mien, Willow got a bit nervous. "We'd better head back for town." Adding, "I'm not feeling so good," when he towered over her in a threatening manner.

Though getting back to town caused her even more distress when she found herself mounted behind Ryder. Sweet heaven, being snugged against him like that was next to outright torture. Lord, she needed to get a life.

"Follow those prints," she told him, spotting Tequila's and the wobbly one's leading away from the stream nearly together, "and maybe we can get some idea of who pushed me into that damn hole."

She didn't miss the bite to his tone when Ryder asked, "You mean you think it might be someone other than me?"

Willow couldn't help herself. "Your horse's shoe isn't loose, right?"

He grunted something that she was certain was obscene under his breath.

But she couldn't help glancing back to check for certain. Judging from the prints, the palomino's shoes were all just fine.

"You want to get a closer look—I'll let you down," he growled.

And he'd probably leave her there to hotfoot it back to Santa Fe alone, Willow thought. "That won't be necessary."

Still, she couldn't help speculating. Ryder could have followed her out to the pueblo ruins, pushed her into the kiva, left with Tequila, and doubled back after seeing Miguel Borrego to establish an alibi. Though he obviously hadn't, not unless he had enough time to get to a blacksmith in between excursions out to the desert, too. And from the position of the sun, Willow didn't think she'd been out that long.

She supposed Ryder could have access to more than one horse, but unless her instincts were too confused by her attraction, Willow was certain Ryder's concern for her was genuine. More likely, one of the vigilantes was responsible. Those three men had reason to want revenge. She remembered the hangman's warning in the Whitiker store. But wasn't trying to kill her for stopping the hanging a bit extreme? Then, again, maybe the one responsible hadn't tried to kill her. Maybe he'd just been trying to scare her off. Willow tried to take comfort in that theory.

The tracks were discernible most of the way to Santa Fe, Tequila's alongside the second set. The person who'd attacked her had to be leading her horse. Straight to Borrego's Stable? Unfortunately, they finally lost the trail among dozens of other horse and wagon prints well before they got into town.

So much for her only hint to her attacker's identity. Willow was still pondering on it when Ryder pulled into the stable. Miguel Borrego was dozing. But their clatter woke him and he popped right up out of his chair.

Eyes wide, he said, "Señorita Kane, you are alive!" and rushed to her side to help her down.

Startled by the acknowledgment—why would Miguel have thought otherwise?—Willow felt the slight tremor of his hands on her waist and noticed him giving Ryder a weird look as she touched down.

Uneasy, she said, "You seem awfully surprised to see me."

"Yes. I mean . . . your horse . . . he came back without you, some cause of concern. I am only happy you are not hurt."

Was she imagining it, or did the stable owner seem downright nervous at her showing up with Ryder? Did he have reason to *want* her dead?

Before Willow had time to contemplate it, Ryder grabbed her wrist. "C'mon." He dragged her toward the street, yelling, "Take good care of Gold Rush." Then, to her, saying, "Let's see to that pretty head of yours."

Tempted to drag her heels just so he didn't think he could boss her, Willow gave over. "I thought you already did. You made it hurt enough."

"Not enough," Ryder said grimly. "Not by a long shot."

RYDER DIDN'T CONSIDER himself a cruel man. Though he might enjoy threatening Willow—or embarrassing her as he had in the saloon the night before—he had no desire to see her in pain. But experience only a few days old told him that he wouldn't have a choice.

Willow had fought his insistence they go to her quarters, but in the end he'd worn her down and she'd given in grudgingly. Entering the room that was much smaller than his suite, Ryder asked, "So, where's your saddlebags?"

"Under the bed."

He reached beneath the bed, found the leather bags and pulled. Then he dropped them on the mattress. "Find those medicines you used on me."

Willow grimaced. "Uh-oh, that's what I was afraid of—payback time."

She certainly used strange words. Had since they'd met. Could be part of her affliction, he guessed, not for a minute forgetting he thought her a bit light in the head. Back to the bags. Realizing she wasn't jumping to his command, Ryder undid one of the buckles himself, only to have her frantically rip the leather from his hands and dive inside.

"I'll get it."

Though her reaction primed his curiosity, Ryder gave over. He'd get a look at what she didn't want him to see soon enough. He could wait until she wasn't paying attention...or at least until she was more fit. Thinking about wrestling her for the saddlebags across the bed piqued his imagination. And made him edgy. He'd been wanting to touch her, despite what his brain told his body.

Instead, he paced the floor while she withdrew the kit he hadn't been able to see well by moonlight. A red cross and the words *First Aid* were printed across the front of a metal box.

From inside, Willow retrieved a bottle and a small pad of material. Sitting on the edge of the bed, she sighed and held them out. "The hydrogen peroxide."

The bubbling solution that had made him think she was practicing witchcraft. Maybe she was. Maybe she'd cast some spell over him. Ryder had never felt so connected with another woman in his life. Since she'd saved him from being hung, Willow crowded his thoughts far too often. He wanted to get closer to her, more personal. He wanted to hold her in his arms and taste her womanliness.

All too aware of the unnatural stiffness of his fingers, he gently parted her hair to find the injury. Had she not used this potion on him, he would have opted for whiskey, a more common answer to stop any festering. He wet the cloth and dabbed the liquid on the raw area. When she winced and sucked air between her teeth, Ryder's own healing wound responded—from memory or in empathy, he wasn't certain—and he couldn't quite hold back a shudder.

"Don't say this hurts you as much as it does me," Willow groused.

Not wanting her to know what power she had over him, Ryder didn't say a word, merely swallowed hard and ignored his suddenly stinging neck. He traded her the bottle for a tube and carefully applied a bit of the ointment.

"You might want to use some more of that," she said.

"The rope burn is healing as it is."

His neck really was on the mend—other than the weird sensation he'd just experienced. He returned the tube to Willow, their fingers touching for an instant. She started and their eyes met and he knew she was as aware of the attraction between them as he. Suddenly looking away, she packed up the medicine kit.

"So, tell me about this younger sister of yours," Ryder said, fighting the thickening of his voice. "Does she run away often?"

"Tansy does crazy things, always has, but she's never run away from home before." Willow sounded breathy, as if still affected by their closeness. "I don't even think she did this time. Not purposely."

"How does anyone run off by accident?"

"Situations can get away from you," she said mysteriously.

How well Ryder knew. He hadn't meant to kill anyone, but he had.

Before he let the nightmare get hold of him, he pushed the issue of Willow's sister. "What about your parents? Are they out searching for Tansy?"

"I don't know. Grandpa's seventy-eight and not doing so well. And Mama...she's never handled stress well, it seems. She wasn't around much when we were growing up. Neither Tansy nor I ever met our fathers, so there's no one else."

Ryder felt her pain at the admission. "At least you and your sister have two people left to love you." He'd lost everyone close to him at too young an age, which was the reason he'd found it so easy to go bad.

"Grandpa Jonah does love Tansy, even though he says she's like Mama," Willow murmured. "Been saying that for a dozen years, since she left us to live with him permanently. Tansy looks like Mama—the red hair and green eyes—and Grandpa's always watched her like a hawk. Always said she took after his wild Audrey. Maybe Tansy set out to prove him right, yet again. I don't know."

Ryder suspected the old man loved his wild Audrey, too. Why else would the old man have raised her daughters?

"So why don't you know what's going on there?" he asked. "I thought you said you checked home."

"I tried." Willow turned her face up to him, and in all seriousness, said, "Home wasn't there—that's the biggest problem."

Ryder frowned. "You're talking in circles." Making him wonder if the head injury wasn't affecting her more than he'd thought.

"Sounds like that, doesn't it?" Willow grimaced and said, "If I told you, you wouldn't believe me. I didn't believe it at first."

To placate her, he said, "Try me."

"Promise you won't tell anyone else . . . or that you won't have me locked up in a loony bin."

Loony bin. What kind of a word was this? Another language? A strange dialect of English? Was she originally from Canada or something?

His gaze meeting her anxious expression, he said, "You have my word."

After which she took a deep breath and mumbled, "I'm not from here," the words all together.

"I know you're not from Santa Fe," he said patiently. "But didn't you say your mother was?"

"Actually, I *am* from Santa Fe. The general area, anyway," Willow quickly added. "Just not in 1885. Tansy disappeared on a day in *1995*. I think she wished herself back here, and when I prayed to find her, I was sent after her."

Ryder felt his chest squeeze with hurt for Willow. "I think that bump on your head is more serious than I thought. Maybe I better get you to a doctor."

"Ryder, you promised! Sit down and listen."

Careful to give her some space, he sat on the mattress. Even so, he was aware of her heat mere inches away. A heat that he would like to have snugged against his flesh. "I'm listening." Not that he figured she was going to make a lick of sense.

"Do you know anything about the pueblo ruins where you found me? About the mesa itself?"

"Mesa Milagro?" Ryder started. "I heard that old legend about some starving Pueblos saving themselves from the Spaniards by up and disappearing."

"Those Indians really did vanish—"

"If you believe legends."

"—right before the Spanish soldiers' eyes," Willow finished.

"So they had a secret way out, maybe the spirit tunnel from the area where you fell."

"Was pushed," she corrected. "If there was a way out, don't you think the Spaniards would have found it? They didn't. That's why they named the place Mesa Milagro. What I've come to believe is that they gathered around their sacred kiva and prayed for safety...no matter how that could be accomplished... and that their prayers were so strong they were granted their wish. I believe they were transported to another time...like Tansy and me."

"An incredible story."

One that made Ryder shift uncomfortably. It simply couldn't be true, but he didn't really want to believe Willow was completely out of her head. She'd been affected by the legend—that had to be it.

"Okay, I guess I've gotta do this."

Willow dug into the saddlebags and spoiled Ryder's fantasies about fighting her for what lay hidden in them. She pulled out a long black tube and, suddenly, a bright light shone from one end. Recognizing it as being the beam that blinded him the other night, he quickly jumped off the bed.

"Is that any way to show gratitude?" he demanded, anger getting the best of him.

"What?" Willow's expression was one of confusion. Then the light dawned over her beautiful features. Her eyes widened. "You thought I was going to hit you again? No. No! I wanted to show you this flashlight." She held it out toward him in a non-threatening way. "Ever seen anything like that before?"

Gingerly he took the thing, handling it as if it were a snake. The beam cast light into the shadows of the room. No heat, though. He passed his hand close to the light. No flame of any kind. Maybe Willow *was* a witch. She dug into the saddlebag again, this time fetching something smaller—a timepiece of sorts.

"This is the latest in what we call wristwatches. Not only does it run on battery—um, you don't have to wind it every day—but look." She pressed a button and the area behind the hands lit a spooky bluish green. "You can tell time no matter how dark the night."

Unsettled, Ryder asked, "Where did you get these things?"

"A hundred and ten years in the future."

But he still wasn't certain she was telling him the truth, not even with the odd timepiece she called a wristwatch and the object she called a flashlight as proof.

"I wish I could make you believe me!" Her features pulled together in frustration.

He was inspecting the timepiece closer now, and spotted a tiny window with a date. "The correct day of the month, but no year," he murmured.

"Wait! What if I could show you something that had the year printed on it . . ." Willow stuck her hand back in the bag and pulled out a small leather case. "Twentieth-century money. Look at the dates."

Willow emptied a compartment onto the bed. Strange-looking coins fell across the coverlet. Then she opened a second compartment and pulled out paper bills. Ryder inspected all carefully as she'd instructed.

The oldest of the coins had been minted in 1974.

The oldest bill printed in 1989.

She really was from the future—if he could believe this was real money rather than counterfeit.

"I know it's a stretch, but you've got to believe me," she urged. "I can't do this alone anymore. Someone's got to believe me!"

Upon which she burst into tears.

And Ryder found himself pulling Willow into his arms. "Either you're telling the truth or you've bewitched me, because I believe you," he admitted, his blood pounding strongly as her softness touched him. "I don't know how it's possible, but I believe . . ."

Willow smiled through her tears, and Ryder was stunned by her beauty. Luminous brown eyes surrounded by sooty lashes, high cheekbones, straight nose, lush mouth.

The mouth got to him as it had earlier. He couldn't help himself. He kissed it more gently than he had the last time. And yet his heart beat just as wildly. He felt the same heat rise from his nether regions. He wanted her. All of her. And unless he was a fool who didn't know up from down, Willow wanted him, as well. Her soft moan told him, as did her body, which moved seductively against his.

The kiss deepened as did his desire for her. His hand trailed to the rounded softness of her breast. He hesitated, then covered the mound, feeling her heart flutter against his fingers. Through the thin cloth, her nipple tightened, making him want to delve beneath the material so he could better touch her.

They were on a bed. Making love would be so easy...so satisfying.

But Willow was in an upheaval because of her situation, because of her sister. He knew how losing family felt. It made a person question everything he was raised to believe.

Ryder didn't know how much of that emotion he sensed in Willow was for him. And when he made love to her, he wanted her to be thinking *only* of him, not of another life, not of fear. He wanted to be more than her solace at being lost in a strange world.

For Willow was lost, Ryder knew.

Just as he was.

And because she was vulnerable, he slid his hand back to her side, the subtle motion sending a desire raging through him. Yet he pushed her gently from him. Too nobly, perhaps. She seemed a bit surprised.

And grateful, he acknowledged.

He pulled back, not for the world wanting to hurt her. But someone had. He wondered if she was thinking of that, for he sensed her renewed tension.

"Do you have any idea of who pushed you into the kiva?" he asked, trying to get his mind off their seductive circumstances, trying to will the swelling in his trousers to desist.

Willow's voice was tight. "It had to be one of the three men I stopped from killing you."

"You saw him?" Ryder wanted to string up the bastard. "What did he look like?"

Willow shook her head. "I didn't see anything. I didn't even know someone was there until seconds before I was pushed. But those three men have to be furious with me, and I can't figure out what motive anyone else might have.''

But Ryder could. ''Ramona.''

''What?''

He himself had been a little uneasy at the vague likeness at first, though getting to know Willow more intimately had brought out the differences for him. He wondered that he'd ever compared the two women, for their resemblance to each other was merely superficial. But that didn't mean that others couldn't be wondering about her.

''Maybe you spooked whoever murdered her....'' Realizing Willow was staring at him oddly, Ryder clenched his jaw. ''You think that could be me.''

''I didn't say that.''

But she'd been thinking it. Wondering. And he guessed he couldn't blame her. But he could be sorely disappointed. Even now she didn't try to reassure him. He'd never been so close to another human being since he was a kid. And yet he'd never felt such a chasm as he did at that moment...when Willow couldn't force herself to tell him she believed in him.

Then again, why should he expect her to, when it had been years since he'd believed in himself? He'd done things she would hate. Better that she have doubts about him anyway. That'd make her keep her distance. She had enough trouble as it was. She didn't need a whole passel more. And if there was one thing he knew how to do...

He was expert on bringing disasters down on innocent people's heads.

Chapter Seven

Willow sensed Ryder's withdrawal. She shouldn't be surprised, considering her ambivalence toward him had to be showing. She only wished she could say the words he undoubtedly wanted to hear.

Instead, she asked, "So, what now?" hoping they could come to some kind of truce.

Peaceful coexistence was probably the best she could expect. She had to repress the growing ache she had for Ryder—the way he made her all riled up inside—and not only because she still had a tiny seed of doubt that he wasn't really what he seemed.

After all, as soon as she found Tansy, she would be headed back to her own time. The uncertainty, along with the exploits of the last few days, had been nerve-racking for a practical woman such as herself. More and more, Willow was looking forward to being reunited with the familiar. Hard work and responsibility were looking better and better to her.

She and Ryder had no future together. She didn't even know why she thought it, except for that kiss. She hadn't resisted because she'd wanted his mouth on hers. A wild, reckless part of herself that she hadn't known existed had wanted him.

"We look after each other's backs," he was saying. "Try to figure out who had it in for Ramona."

He was telling her he was innocent. She mostly believed him, *wanted* to believe him, certainly. And Ramona's death seemed to be affecting both of them. It wouldn't hurt to do a little probing for both their sakes, as long as it didn't interfere with her search for Tansy.

Returning the saddlebags beneath the bed, she said, "You think it's Cal Atchley, right?" Willow hadn't forgotten the set-to Ryder'd had with the man at the card table. And the vigilantes had been Atchley's men.

Ryder nodded. "Ramona made Atchley her personal customer. The night before she died, I saw them arguing on the street."

"How 'personal' was their relationship?"

"Good question, especially since she and Miguel Borrego were lovers," Ryder mused. "And Atchley has a wife. Sickly woman. He bought her a house here in town. Maybe he needed more lively company and wanted to take Borrego's place."

"Or maybe Atchley already did and the fact didn't get around. And since Borrego moonlights here playing the guitar for Benita, he might have put two and two together," Willow added.

"And he wouldn't have been pleased with Ramona's attentions to some rich cattle rancher," Ryder finished for her.

"Would Borrego have taken his jealousy out on Cal Atchley... or on the woman he loved?"

Realizing they'd arrived at a second suspect, Willow grabbed the iron bedstead. They stared at each other in stunned silence for a moment. Surely solving a murder couldn't be this easy.

Then Ryder said, "Maybe we oughta find out exactly how close Ramona and Atchley did get."

"Hazel might know," Willow said. "Or maybe something here in Ramona's room could tell us."

"You haven't gone through her belongings?"

"I've been busy with other things."

"Like getting yourself into trouble," Ryder said, his tone light. "Now's as good a time as any."

Not that there was much to go through. The room was simple, small, without a nook or cranny to check. Her own things were under the bed. That left the dresser.

They searched one drawer at a time, Ryder too close for her comfort. Every time they touched, she felt a sense of expectancy that was totally new to her. And disturbing.

The first drawer held hair ornaments and a few pieces of jewelry.

The second was filled with serviceable undergarments and naughty lingerie worthy of a modern-day Victoria's Secret shop. Willow was a bit embarrassed seeing Ryder handle the garments with some interest. She wondered if he was thinking about *her* wearing them. She knew she was, and the thought made her blush even as her insides warmed and flowered.

The third drawer held only a *rebozo,* a woven wool wrap, and she clung to the harsh material to center herself.

"Nothing that tells us anything about Ramona," Ryder said.

"Unless . . ." Willow picked up the Bible. "I guess this tells us she was religious."

"Catholic."

"That probably meant she went to confession."
Willow thought about the Santuario de Guadelupe,
not that it was the only Catholic church in town.

"A priest doesn't share his parishioners' confessions," Ryder said.

"Not even after she's dead, if it were to help find
her killer?"

Willow opened the Bible, as if it could offer up an
answer. She glanced at the notations about the Cruz
family, originally from Albuquerque, a larger city to
the south. The Bible had belonged first to Ramona's
mother, who had made notations about births and
deaths in the family—or, more likely, had asked the
local priest to do so, since it was doubtful that someone of low economic means knew how to write.

"Ramona was the oldest of seven children," Willow said. "It seems she inherited the Bible after her
mother's death a few years back." About to close the
book, she hesitated, then took a better look at the only
entry following the older woman's date of demise, after Ramona would have inherited the Bible. The
handwriting was different. "Did you know Ramona
lost her brother Emilio about six months ago, right
here in Santa Fe?"

Ryder shook his head. "That was about the time
Ramona came to town herself."

"Could there be a connection?"

"Hard to say. Maybe we should find out more
about Emilio Cruz and how he died."

"That calls for a trip to the sheriff's office."

Having checked her watch before putting it away,
Willow figured she had about enough time to do so
and get back for supper. She replaced the Bible on the
dresser, then fastened her hair with Tansy's clip, real-

izing through the reflection in the mirror that Ryder was watching her every movement. A tingling spread through her and she felt a bit breathless.

"You shouldn't be going anywhere but to bed," Ryder told her, his voice deep and resonant.

Glancing over her shoulder, Willow raised her brows at what could easily be misconstrued as a double entendre. A shiver of desire coursed through her.

"I meant to rest," he added, but she wasn't so certain.

"Sure you did." Breasts tightening as she brushed by him, she mumbled, "Let's go."

The sheriff's office was on another of the streets just off the plaza. Filled with a sense of purpose, ignoring the attraction to Ryder she couldn't forget, Willow entered with him following...seemingly reluctant. She wondered if he had no use for the law or for Sheriff Landry, specifically. Then, again, he might have reservations coming here, considering some of the townspeople had been determined to see him pay for Ramona's death.

Sheriff Landry was sound asleep on the job, leaning back in his office chair, muddy boots propped up on the desk, grease-stained hat pulled low over his face. A single prisoner in the jail cell behind him was stretched out on his bunk, snoring.

Ryder hit one of Landry's feet and, when the sheriff came to with a start, growled, "Sorry to disturb your afternoon nap."

Feet flying off the desk, hat righted in a second, Landry went pale when he saw Ryder. Willow was unimpressed by the man's appearance—his shirt so tight across his paunch that the buttons looked ready to burst, the cloth stained with what probably had been his lunch.

"Heard you had some trouble coupla days ago," he said to Ryder.

"Yeah, and you're right on the case. Not that I expected you to come see me—forget arresting the men who tried to string me up."

"I been busy." Landry shuffled the papers on his desk as if he actually meant to do something with them. He gave them a sour grin. "And no harm done, far as I kin tell. So what can I do fer you folks today?"

Thinking the sheriff probably feared that Ryder would insist he look into the vigilantes, Willow figured he'd feel let off the hook when she said, "Tell us about Emilio Cruz."

"Who?"

Ryder impatiently explained. "Emilio Cruz died here in Santa Fe about six months ago."

"Cruz," Landry echoed. "Cruz. Oh, yeah, he was one of them bank robbers."

"He got shot robbing a bank?" Willow asked.

"Nope. Got away. Mighta been gone for good if not for Madrid."

Her knees nearly buckled. "Wolf Madrid?"

"You heard of him, then. Yeah, Madrid's the best bounty hunter this side of the Mississippi."

Ryder was staring at her intently when he said, "So this Madrid brought Cruz in dead, rather than alive."

"Nope. Cruz was alive, all right. Dumb thing, him tryin' to escape. Got my deputy's gun and fired it at Madrid. That's when Madrid took him out. Instinct, you know. Didn't even have time to think and that gun was in his hand and blastin' away." Sauntering over to the front door, Landry sounded as if he admired Wolf Madrid. "He only wounded Cruz, though. Kid shoulda lived. Doc Travis got to him in time, said the wound wasn't serious. But a coupla days later, Cruz sickened and died. Weirdest thing."

Considering the unsophisticated state of medicine in the nineteenth century, Willow didn't think Cruz's dying of complications sounded so weird. "Did you know Emilio Cruz and Ramona Cruz were brother and sister?"

Landry didn't answer. He was too busy staring out to the street. He cursed under his breath.

"Ah, I just know they're headin' fer this office. Now they're goin' to ruin another day fer me!"

"Who?"

"Them Whitikers. Since they moved to town and bought the general store last fall, they been on my back constantly. Expect me to clean up the entire town so good, moral folks, like them, can sleep safe at night!"

Exactly what the good people of Santa Fe were paying him to do, Willow thought, not that she commented. Not wanting a second run-in with Titus in one day, she thought it prudent they leave.

"I don't think we're going to learn anything else here," she said to Ryder. "And if I don't hurry back, I'll miss supper."

"Good thinking," Landry agreed, locking gazes with Ryder. "They see you here, who knows what'll come down on both our heads. Git while the goin's good."

Ryder didn't argue, merely tightened his jaw and pulled his hat low on his forehead. Willow peeked out the window and saw Titus and Velma, the handle of a covered picnic basket over her arm. They'd stopped down the street and were engrossed in conversation with Cal Atchley. What did they have to do with the rancher? Shrugging it off as business—and maybe a little poker-playing camaraderie between the two men—Willow slipped out of the sheriff's office.

With Ryder following close behind, she chose a circuitous route down a side street so they wouldn't have to face Titus Whitiker. A tense silence grew between them.

Then, a block from the Red Mesa Saloon, Ryder asked, "You know this Wolf Madrid?"

Odd question. And an odd inflection in Ryder's voice, Willow decided. "I know *of* him. And I ran into him at the general store this morning. Why?"

"Just curious. I was wondering how you knew a bounty hunter at all, considering you say you came from the future."

"I *did* come from the future," she said in a low enough voice that passersby couldn't overhear. "And I've seen enough dime novels about Madrid to know who he is."

"That trash still exists in the next century?" Ryder sounded disgusted.

Being that her ancestor wrote the stories, Willow took exception to his critical tone. "They're very entertaining." Or at least she'd have to take Tansy's word on it, since Willow had never been interested enough in the Wild West to pick one up.

"They can ruin a man, as well."

Willow gave Ryder the benefit of the doubt on that one, since she'd once read that dime novels were kind of equivalent to modern-day unauthorized biographies in that they exaggerated the more flashy parts of one's life. Rarely did the unauthorized biographies emphasize the positive about the person whose story they were telling, however. On the other hand, she was certain the Wolf Madrid novels made him out to be a hero, so Ryder had to be referring to someone else's story.

She thought to ask him about it, when they passed a darkly handsome man standing in a recessed doorway and staring at her. The man reminded her of Wolf, somewhat. Willow was certain he was part Indian, though he cut his hair and dressed like a white man—all but for the moccasins on his feet. Looking into his chiseled face, Willow had the sensation she'd seen him somewhere before. But where? She felt his gaze follow her across the street. But when she glanced over her shoulder, the stranger was gone. Vanished.

Ryder stopped at the entrance to the saloon. "Got some business to take care of over in Burro Alley," he said. "While I'm there, I'll ask around about your sister."

Willow swallowed hard. "Thanks." Though she wanted to find Tansy desperately, she wasn't thrilled at the prospect of her sister showing up there. She knew enough of Santa Fe's history to realize Burro Alley was, among other things, a red-light district of the time. She herself needed to lie down for a few minutes, since her head was pounding. "I'll catch you later," she called after Ryder, who was already on his way.

Ryder just kept on going.

And Willow told herself she simply couldn't be feeling lonesome because he'd left her. She had the blues, all right, but they had nothing to do with Ryder Smith.

They couldn't.

"HOW ABOUT YOU AND ME step out together sometime?" Farley Garnett suggested to Willow.

During all three of his breaks that evening, the flirtatious dealer sought her company and tried to weave some kind of a spell over her. Even through her distraction—wondering when Ryder would walk in, what he had discovered—Willow realized it. Not that she took Farley seriously.

"I don't know that I'll be around long enough to make that possible," she said truthfully.

She glanced over at two of the poker players who'd been studiously ignoring each other. Both Titus Whitiker and Cal Atchley had been playing all night. But they sat opposite each other at the table, and not once had she heard them exchange words other than about the game. Even now, during the break, they kept their distance, Atchley jawing with a couple of cowboys, Titus sitting alone, stacking and restacking his poker chips obsessively.

Had the men had a disagreement when she'd seen them that afternoon? Or were they trying hard to seem as though they weren't friendly?

"Are you sure it's not Smith keeping you from saying yes?" Farley asked her, his smile fading.

If she were in any situation to consider Farley's offer of company, that might apply. But since that wasn't the case, she replied, "Ryder Smith doesn't run me."

"Haven't seen you with any other man."

When had he seen them together at all other than here at the saloon? Coming from the sheriff's office? On the street the night before? At the pueblo ruins? Now she was really reaching. She had no reason to suspect Farley Garnett.

"We're friendly," she said.

"Good friends?"

"Maybe."

Scowling outright, Farley shook his head. "Watch your step around Smith, Willow. Don't get too involved. He's more'n a card shark...and he's plenty dangerous."

"In what way?" She expected him to refer to Ryder's gunmanship.

Instead, Farley said, "Look what happened to Ramona."

Making Willow uneasy. "Ryder wasn't involved with Ramona."

"That what he told you?"

Willow swallowed hard. Mere hours ago, she and Ryder had speculated about Ramona's relationships with Cal Atchley and Miguel Borrego. Not once had Ryder hinted that he'd had any kind of acquaintance with Ramona outside of the saloon. The implication made her tremble inside, and made her head start to ache once more.

"You think he killed her, too?" Did the whole town believe that?

"I'm the one who recognized Smith's lucky poker chip Atchley pried outa her hand."

Not that that meant anything, Willow told herself, though she'd conveniently forgotten about the physical evidence that had stirred three men to an impromptu hanging.

"He doesn't let those chips out of his sight," Farley added. "How else do you think she got hold of one?"

Willow didn't have a clue.

Only later, when Farley was back at the table dealing, did it register that he'd said Atchley was the one to find Ryder's lucky poker chip in Ramona's hand. What if Atchley had somehow sneaked a chip off the poker table, killed Ramona, then tried to set Ryder up for the murder, even going so far as to send his boys to do the hanging?

As if she'd conjured him, Ryder entered the saloon, but he didn't so much as look her way. His attention was focused on the poker table and the one remaining seat.

Willow clenched her jaw in frustration when he went for it, making himself comfortable, taking a short stack of silver-trimmed black chips from his vest and setting them in front of him. The famous lucky chips. Then he threw money at the dealer to buy game chips.

Why hadn't he sought her out first, told her what he'd learned? Why didn't he seem to want her company as much as she wanted his?

The minutes crawled like hours, the hours like days. Ryder lost some hands, won more. Both Atchley and Titus glared daggers at the man, but neither started anything.

Finally, when Willow was so exhausted she could barely keep her eyes open, Hazel announced, "Ten minutes until closing, boys. Last call if you're thirsty."

Over at the poker table, Ryder scooped the pot of chips toward himself, then settled with Farley, trading them for bills and coins.

And Willow waited tensely as Ryder returned his lucky chips to his vest pocket. Then he shoved the money into a coat pocket and rose, straightening his hat.

Was he just going to up and leave, for heaven's sake?

To her relief, Ryder headed her way. "Let's go upstairs to my suite," he said in a low voice.

Tension curled in the pit of Willow's stomach at his hard expression. He must have learned something she wasn't going to like. That's why he'd waited all this time to tell her. Her personal interest waning, she led the way upstairs.

A lit, cut-crystal lamp and low fire awaited them in Ryder's sitting room. She perched gingerly on the red upholstered sofa, while he threw himself into the chair opposite.

"What did you find out?" she asked above the pounding of her heart.

"Something that doesn't make sense about your story." His blue gaze bored into her.

Immediately on the defensive, Willow demanded, "Like what?"

"Like I found someone who recognized your description of Tansy, down to her wearing men's clothes like yours... but he said he hadn't seen the girl in months."

"Months? I don't understand. Could we have arrived in the same year, but at different times?" She supposed it was possible—anything seemed to be. Only guessing what her sister might have gone through these past weeks, Willow felt like crying again. "Where could she have disappeared to?"

"More important, why would she be calling herself Audrey Kane?" Ryder asked.

Willow gaped. "Audrey is our mother!"

"I remember."

"Tansy's going around using Mama's name?" That had to be it, Willow told herself.

Because either Tansy was pretending to be Mama... or Mama had found the chink in time before them.

FROM WILLOW'S STUNNED expression, Ryder knew she was thinking the same thing he had when the red-haired, green-eyed teenager had been identified as Audrey, rather than Tansy, Kane.

"All those times Mama up and disappeared for days or weeks when I was small... it's possible, I suppose." She was talking more to herself than to him. "Could Grandpa Jonah have known? When did it start? When she was a wild teenager? Is that what Grandpa feared when he kept bemoaning how Tansy reminded him of her?"

"If your mother really was here, at least you know she got back to your own time, and you can, too."

Something Ryder didn't want to consider—he was getting used to having Willow around. But he couldn't even comprehend the complexities of having generations of Kane women racing back and forth through the centuries. He just barely believed this time travel was possible to begin with.

"Gives you something to think about, doesn't it?" he muttered darkly.

"I'll have plenty of time to think after I find Tansy and get her home." She fiddled with the silver-and-turquoise clip holding her hair to the side. "She has to be here somewhere."

"And we'll figure out where," Ryder said with more certainty than he was feeling. Once you knew the rules could be broken, how could a person be certain of anything? "It's just a matter of patience and persistence."

Willow turned a grateful if fleeting smile on him. "We will find her... and clear you."

"I'm not important."

When he'd suggested they watch each other's backs, Ryder had done so for Willow's sake, so nothing would happen to her before she could escape back to her own time. He was used to taking care of himself. And if bad luck caught up to him, then he was only getting what he deserved, anyway. A man could only run from his fate for so long.

"You *are* important," she murmured. "To me."

Gazing into Willow's eyes, Ryder caught a glimmer of something fleeting, yet breathtaking—the sensation of what it would be like to be loved again. But all too soon he would lose her as he had every person who'd ever meant anything to him. He couldn't count on her being around long, and he knew it. Why did the realization make him ache so? At least she wouldn't die like the others... though she would still be out of his reach and, therefore, dead to him.

Unable to accept that, he drew her to him, to his heart, and held her there for what seemed like forever. But forever was a long, long time. Forever was an interminable life without her. She was clutching his arms, shuddering against him. Ryder pulled back slightly, touched her face. Willow's eyes shone. Her expression was open...inviting.

Scooping her face between both hands, he kissed her forehead, her cheek, her mouth, each brush of his lips against her flesh sending his emotions careening. He wanted her more than any woman he'd ever had. But he couldn't have her. He knew that. No matter what he did, he couldn't bind her to him. She might care about him, but her loyalties lay elsewhere, with her family...her sister. He understood. He let go of her.

Clearing his throat, he tried to be practical. "We'd better concentrate on Tansy. Finding both your sister and a killer in the short time you'll be here isn't likely."

"We can try." Before he could object, she said, "I'm involved. I involved myself when I saved you from a hanging," she reminded him, as if he ever could forget. "And someone tried to hurt me because I did."

"Maybe if you stay out of it, he'll leave you alone."

"That's not likely, either." She sighed. "I've been thinking, the horse we followed back here had a loose shoe."

"I remember," he said dryly. How could he forget her suspicious nature?

"Someone had to fix the shoe. How many blacksmith shops does Santa Fe have?"

"At least a couple. I never counted."

"We can check them out tomorrow, while we continue asking around about Tansy."

They could ask every blacksmith they found if he'd fixed a single shoe. Ryder knew how exhausted Willow must be—searching for her sister, falling into the kiva, working all night—but she seemed ready to start again right now. When she finally allowed herself to let go. . .

"Sounds like we'll have a busy day tomorrow and that you should hit your bunk."

Willow rose from the sofa. "You're right, of course. I only hope I *can* sleep."

As did Ryder. Rather, he wished Willow could sleep in his arms, that he could savor every minute of her before she vanished from his life forever. Though if she *were* in his arms, he doubted either one of them would sleep at all. He would make love to her the whole night long.

And that would be wrong.

For Willow Kane belonged to some man in the future, not to him.

Chapter Eight

"Why hasn't anyone seen her?" Willow muttered as she and Ryder backtracked toward the Red Mesa Saloon after a full day of wandering Santa Fe's streets. Her search for her sister had been as fruitless as ever. If only she could figure out some other way to find Tansy. "Or a horse with a loose shoe?"

"Patience."

"I've *been* patient. I want results."

They'd tried two blacksmith shops to no avail. Neither man had taken care of a horse with a single loose shoe.

Someone had.

She was losing it. Having slept in fits and starts, having spent half the night imagining her mother walking these very streets as a teenager herself, Willow was feeling a bit brittle. Other, more complicated, notions had occurred to her—like her mother being only eighteen and alone when she'd been born. Grandpa Jonah had surmised that some drifter had seduced his daughter and walked out on her before even knowing she was in the family way, though Mama had insisted she'd been well acquainted with and had been wildly in love with Willow's father.

Willow wondered if there wasn't more to the story—like her mother becoming enamored with a man she'd met here in the past. That certainly would explain why her father had never been around.

Usually Willow managed to keep her resentment toward Mama in check—unlike Tansy—but at the moment, bitterness blossomed, full-blown. Lots of kids were raised in single-parent homes, but normally they knew their other parent, had a relationship of some kind. But Audrey Kane had not only withheld the identities of both her and Tansy's fathers all these years, she'd hardly been a parent herself. Willow had never called her on it either, rather she'd kept her hurt bottled up, had tucked it away as if it didn't matter.

But it did matter.

She hated lies and secrets, and Mama was guilty of both.

Ryder interrupted her musings. "Let's try Jacob Hansen's over there, then get you back to Red Mesa before you miss supper."

Already late, Willow grumbled her agreement. Getting worked up over what she couldn't change would do her no good.

Heat poured out of the smithy even before they stepped through the open doors. Jacob Hansen worked before the forge. He was a tall man, brawny enough to fill a doorway. Sweat stained the shirt above his heavy leather apron. His muscles bulged as he hammered heated metal to shape the end of a branding iron.

"Can we have a moment of your time?" Willow asked.

"I'm listening." He didn't stop working, however.

Willow glanced over at the farrier's tools lying around—iron horseshoes and nails, hoof nippers and a steel leather punch. "Did someone bring in a horse yesterday?"

"I'm a blacksmith, ain't I?"

"A horse that needed only one shoe fixed," Ryder clarified.

Hansen finally scrutinized them, his eyes narrowing. "What's it to you?"

"It's personal," Willow said. "And very, very important."

Hansen looked her up and down, nodded to himself. "No secret, anyhow. The horse threw the shoe on the way back into town."

Realizing they'd struck pay dirt, Willow could barely keep the excitement out of her voice when she asked, "Who brought the horse in?"

"Stable owner by the name of Borrego."

Miguel Borrego, one of their suspects! Willow and Ryder exchanged looks.

"Was it one of Borrego's rentals?" Ryder queried.

"Wouldn't know." Hansen waved them off and returned to his task. "Go ask him."

"What did the horse look like?" Willow persisted, even realizing the man seemed short fused. "Please?"

"A big bay gelding."

"Thanks," she said.

"Nice doing business with you."

Willow didn't miss the irony in the man's tone. Skirting a set of wagon wheels, they quickly left the smithy.

"Miguel Borrego," she murmured. "It fits."

"It could be anyone who uses his stable. He could have been seeing to a customer's horse."

"Easy enough to find out, right?"

"If he chooses to tell the truth, which he won't if *he's* the one."

"He could just pin it on anyone," Willow realized. "So how do we find out for sure?"

"I'll try to find out tonight," Ryder said. "While Miguel is playing guitar at the saloon, I'll come back to the stable, take a look at the horses and see if a big bay gelding has a new shoe."

And then they would be able to find out who owned the horse, and who'd pushed her into the kiva, Willow thought with satisfaction...and quite possibly the identity of a murderer.

TOO BAD MIGUEL BORREGO threw a wrench into their plans by not showing up at the saloon that night.

"Benita doesn't have any idea where he is," Amabelle Nelson told Willow. "She's taking it awfully personally. Look at her..." She indicated the Mexican woman, who stiffly paced near the stage where the pretty Ottilie was singing a French tune. "...she's ready to throw a fit."

"So what's new about that?" her twin, Rosabelle, asked.

The blondes giggled as they went off together to deliver a single tray of drinks to some thirsty customers. Only then did Ryder saunter over to Willow, for the moment stationed at the bar.

She looked around to make certain no one would overhear them. They were clear for a few moments—all the girls on the floor were busy, and Hazel and the bartender were engaged in a lively debate with a couple of the regulars down at the other end of the bar.

"What now?" Willow asked in a conspiratorial tone.

"We wait. I can't exactly walk into the stable and check over horses' hooves with Borrego looking on."

"If he's even there." That they had a lead they couldn't follow ate at Willow. "I hate this not knowing."

"Patience," he reminded her, sauntering off when Benita returned to the bar and slammed her drink tray down.

"Alex, two whiskeys!" she called to the bartender.

The dancer's face was wreathed in a scowl and she began muttering to herself in Spanish. Willow was certain she heard the name *Miguel* surrounded by what sounded like a variety of heated curses and chose to take advantage of the dancer while she was off-balance.

"You're in a cheery mood."

Benita flashed her a black look. "What if I am?"

Willow fabricated a deeply sympathetic expression. "You know, you're not the only woman who's been dumped on by a man who makes her heart beat fast."

Benita frowned as if trying to follow Willow's lingo. Then, brow clearing, she said, "Miguel Borrego can go to hell, for all I care!"

And Willow knew she had Benita. Determined to get what she could out of the woman, she said, "Sounds like you've got it bad. Like you're crazy about the man. Give him the benefit of the doubt. He probably feels the same about you."

"I thought he would, after Ramona..."

"After?" Willow echoed, silently finishing, *After Ramona was murdered.*

"Never mind."

The bartender delivered the full shot glasses and Benita indicated he should set them down. She was trembling, trying to get hold of herself.

Wondering if she'd heard the slightest touch of guilt in Benita's tone, Willow pressed her. "Maybe Miguel just needs time to get over Ramona. He did love her, right?"

"She didn't deserve his love! He treated her like she was better than the rest of us. Well, Ramona Cruz wasn't a saint like he thought!"

"She cheated on him with other men?" *Ryder?* Willow wanted to ask. She hadn't forgotten Farley's insinuation.

"Ramona was a cheat, yes. She was deceitful through and through. And money hungry. She'd do anything to get it. Room and board and tips weren't enough for her."

"You mean she took men upstairs?"

"Not regularly...but someone. I heard and I know it wasn't Miguel." Benita's eyes narrowed. "Ramona played up to the men playing poker, acted as a decoy for Farley so he could cheat customers with marked cards and give her a cut."

"What customers? Ryder?"

Benita laughed. "Ramona wouldn't have dared try her tricks on Ryder Smith. He's far too shrewd. But Cal Atchley and Titus Whitiker are both fools."

"I wouldn't go bad-mouthing customers who tip big," Hazel suggested, making them both jump.

Willow's heart raced. How much had Hazel heard? And Benita quickly retreated, whiskeys in hand.

"I get the feeling there was no love lost between Ramona and Benita."

"They were rivals in everything that counted. Both danced for the customers, always trying to outdo one another. And both wanted Miguel Borrego."

"Did Ramona know Benita was after her man?"

"Hah! They had a hair-pulling, nail-gouging fight over him a coupla weeks ago. And Benita pulled a knife on Ramona."

"She cut her?"

"Not then."

"Another time?" Willow pressed.

Hazel lifted her brows. "You know how Ramona died, don't you?"

Startled, Willow had to admit, "No. No one told me any details except the thing about finding Ryder's lucky chip in her hand. I guess I figured she was shot."

Hazel's maroon curls shook. "Stabbed to death," she said, leaving her station to check on her customers.

And leaving Willow to wonder if Benita had killed Ramona in a fit of passion over Miguel.

Another suspect.

WILLOW SHARED the thought with Ryder later, and he didn't dismiss the possibility, though it seemed Sheriff Landry had—if he was even investigating.

Ryder told her he still meant to carry through with his plan to check out the stable, figuring Miguel would have retreated to his shack in back of the barn by then. He wanted to borrow Willow's flashlight; Willow insisted on going with him.

Having changed into her men's clothes, she stuck the flashlight in her waistband and let the vest drop over it. "At least we can see what we're doing now."

"I never shoulda let you fast-talk me into letting you come with me."

"You didn't have a choice if you wanted the flashlight," she said, leading the way from the hall to the outside stairs.

"I should have been satisfied with a lantern."

"So you could let anyone passing by know someone was in the barn? The flashlight is more discreet."

"But comes with a price."

Insulted, Willow said, "Doesn't everything?"

They argued in low voices, though no one seemed to be around to hear. Anyone who wanted action at this hour was over in Burro Alley. That area never closed down.

They approached Borrego's Stable cautiously. The barn was dark. Ryder put a hand on Willow's arm to stop her. No matter that she'd insinuated herself into this night adventure, he was clearly taking charge.

"You wait here while I make certain that Borrego isn't inside. If everything is quiet, I'll act as lookout, while you check all the rear right shoes of every bay in the barn. You can do that, can't you?"

"Which part do you think is too difficult for me to handle?" she asked sarcastically. "Making a horse pick up his foot, or figuring out which one is the rear right?"

"I meant the *wait here* part," he whispered harshly. "Patience is not one of your virtues."

Willow narrowed her gaze on Ryder's retreating back, but she stayed put in the shadows. The corral was empty but for a couple of buggies, Borrego's shack in the back dark. Ryder entered the unlocked barn, and she could hear him call out for Borrego—just loud enough to get the man's attention if he was around. A moment later, Ryder reappeared and gave her the high sign. Swallowing hard, heart pounding, Willow slipped inside.

"I'll keep watch," he said.

"What if someone does come by?"

"I'll signal and you slip out the side door."

Wondering how Ryder would explain *his* presence if caught, Willow got to work in the first stall that held a bay, and with a quick flash of her light, checked to make certain it was a gelding. Murmuring sweet nothings so he wouldn't be startled, she slid her hand down the gelding's leg as if she were going to pick the hoof clean. A little pressure and the horse adjusted its weight so she could lift his foot. Only then did she snap on the flashlight again. The shoe was well-worn. She doused the light and went on.

As she worked her way down the first row of stalls, Willow realized she was stimulated, as she had been for the past few days.

With each worn shoe she found, her sense of expectancy increased.

The realization that she was, in some strange way, enjoying herself, hit Willow full force about the time she got to Ryder's palomino, Gold Rush, who whickered at her softly. She rubbed his rump and went on.

The next bay had a new right rear shoe, and for a moment, her excitement grew, but upon further inspection, she found that the other three were new, as well.

Her excitement deflated but not vanquished, Willow wondered what was happening to her. Spotting a half-empty liquor bottle in the hay, she set it outside the stall where the animal couldn't trounce it and be hurt by broken glass. Then she crossed to the other side of the barn and started anew, her mind racing.

For a woman who didn't have an adventurous bone in her body, she was certainly getting off on playing detective. It wasn't the doing, she told herself, but the goal—catching a probable murderer—that had her juices flowing. Once he was taken care of, she could figure out what black hole had swallowed Tansy and wouldn't have to look over her shoulder while doing so. Once reunited with her sister, Willow told herself, she would be glad to return to her uneventful, work-filled life.

Wouldn't she?

A barn owl mocked her as she snapped off her flashlight.

She wouldn't be glad to see the last of Ryder, of that she was certain. But there was no helping it.

Willow dropped the horse's foot she'd been inspecting, passed by Tequila with a soft greeting and went on to the next stall holding a bay.

The barn owl hooted again.

A quick look revealed another new shoe. Wondering if she would find three more of the same, she inspected the horse's front foot. This shoe was much older, more worn, than the first. Her heart thudded as she clicked off the flashlight, intent on getting a look at the horse's other front hoof. A louder thud came from outside the stall, followed by a flurry of movement that made the horse complain and thrash to the side.

Before Willow could react, she found herself face-down on the stall floor, a hand over her mouth, a body enveloping her. A familiar body.

Ryder!

Then she heard it—the scuffling coming from the other end of the barn. Someone was inside!

So why hadn't Ryder signaled her?

Now it was too late to escape, she thought, hearing the scuffle move closer, followed by a low muttering in Spanish—Borrego, sounding as if he'd been drinking. Her view was obstructed, but she nevertheless saw a soft light swinging close.

He was carrying a lantern.

Willow's heart raced as the golden pool drew closer. It would be just their luck if Borrego had come to fetch the gelding in this stall....

But the stable owner weaved past them, talking to himself. "Now where the hell did I leave it?"

Willow became more aware of the weight on her, not that Ryder was hurting her. Their closeness was unnerving, however, even more so than the danger. Building tension unsettled Willow, and her discomfort grew as Ryder shifted, his knee landing between her thighs.

A multitude of unwanted physical sensations assaulting her, Willow swallowed hard.

"There you are!"

She thought they were caught... but Borrego was only now staggering back the way he came, the pool of swaying light preceding him. She peered through the bay's legs and spotted the object of his search—he was carrying the half-empty bottle of liquor she'd moved out of the stall across the way. Hopefully, he didn't mean to continue his binge here in the barn. She held her breath, waiting.

A moment later, the barn door creaked, and Willow heard him leave, thank goodness. Now she could breathe normally... or as normally as a woman could with a man on top of her.

"That was close," Ryder whispered, his warm breath and mustache feathering the side of her face.

A thrill shot through her, heating her insides.

She thought he was about to kiss her. Tempted to let him, she knew this wasn't the time to be distracted. She fought the inner excitement that sparked everywhere his body touched hers, fought the drugging passion that flared more quickly than she imagined possible.

"*Too* close," Willow gasped, pushing at him until he slid off her, then aching with longing at the separation. Every inch of her that he'd touched quivered. "What's the big idea of tackling me? What happened to that signal you were supposed to send me?"

"I did signal you. *Twice.*" He followed the assurance with a soft hooting sound.

A flush of embarrassment shot through her. "I thought you were a barn owl, for heaven's sake!"

"What did you expect? That I'd whistle?"

Feeling foolish, little flames still kindling inside her, Willow rose, looking for a way out of this conversation. The horse, of course. She zeroed in on the gelding's left front leg and snapped on her flashlight.

"I thought you knew front from back," Ryder said, now sounding amused.

Did he think his effect on her was so great that she didn't know what she was doing? *Arrogant jerk!* It took all her will to keep from telling him so.

"I found a new shoe on this guy. The right front is worn." She inspected the third hoof. "Two worn ones and counting." A thrill of a different kind shooting through her, she moved to the rear left leg. The moment the light touched the shoe, she said, "Bingo!"

"Who?"

"The horse we've been looking for! Now we have to figure out whether or not he's one of Borrego's rentals."

"Give me that."

Realizing he meant the flashlight, Willow tossed it to him. "I thought you were supposed to be playing sentry." Instead he was taking over again, sweeping the stall with light.

"I doubt Borrego'll be back."

"Someone else could find us here," she returned.

Engrossed in his inspection, Ryder grunted. Then the beam stilled and he motioned for her to move closer. "Here, on the noseband." The big bay was trying to bob his head away from the light, but Ryder firmly held on to the halter.

Willow saw the shiny metal plate on the aging narrow leather band that wrapped around the horse's nose.

"That's our owner," he said, tapping a finger against the fancy monogrammed initials.

"T.W.," Willow murmured. The name tumbled from her lips. "Titus Whitiker."

"I don't get it. What does he have against you?"

"The day after I came to your rescue, I was in the store talking to his wife. He came in with one of the vigilantes, who recognized me and told him what I'd done. Titus lost his temper and threw me out. He thinks you're guilty."

Ryder snapped off the flashlight and led her from the stall. "That doesn't make sense."

"His thinking you killed Ramona?"

"That Whitiker'd get so fired up over my not being hung." Ryder lowered his voice to a near whisper as they approached the barn doors. "I mean, there's no love lost between us, but he's been tolerating playing at the same poker table with me for months."

"Remember Sheriff Landry saying the Whitikers have been on his back to clean up the town? Maybe it's just a matter of his being a moralizer."

"I'm not all that sure about Titus Whitiker's convictions, considering he's at the Red Mesa a coupla nights a week. And if he was full of good intentions, he wouldn't try to hurt you. No, if he's involved in any way, the reason would have to be more personal."

Willow thought about what she'd learned earlier. "Benita said Ramona flirted with Titus, as well as with Cal Atchley, to give the house the advantage."

"That woulda been hard to miss," he admitted. "But as far as Whitiker's having some special affection for Ramona, I never noticed it going beyond the game. Not like it did with Atchley, anyhow."

"You'd know better than I would."

Willow felt a bit dejected. So the horse belonged to Titus Whitiker. What motive did he have? Without a motive, they couldn't assume he was either the murderer or her attacker. Miguel Borrego was a stronger suspect. And Borrego did have easy access to Titus Whitiker's horse.

Nearing the door that Borrego had left cracked, Ryder stopped Willow and snaked toward the opening. He peered out into the night for a moment.

"All clear," he murmured, and she caught up with him.

They left the barn together and hurried down the street toward their rooms, Ryder's hand settled in the middle of Willow's back beneath her vest. The warmth imprinted through the thin cotton of her shirt melted her, and she swayed, allowing her body to rest along his as they walked.

When they arrived at her door, Ryder tipped his hat and started to back off. Acting on instinct, Willow grabbed him by the ruffles on his shirt and stood on her toes to brush a kiss across his mouth. The soft bristle of his mustache made her nerves stand on end.

The warmth of his lips made her insides tumble. But when he stepped closer, she stopped him from taking her in his arms. Her instinct for self-preservation warred with her desire for a man she couldn't have for more than a few days.

Getting too close to him would be a big mistake.

For the more intimate she and Ryder got, the harder separating would be.

WHAT IN BLUE BLAZES was Ramona up to now?

She wants to find you, a little voice said. She wants to point a finger at the person who tried to kill her.

That had to be it. Ramona was out for revenge and had to be stopped. Each day she was allowed to live, she grew more dangerous. Throwing her into that pit had been a stroke of genius. No one should ever have found her, not until everything had rotted but her bones.

So how had she gotten herself out if not with help?

Help. He had freed her. And now she wasn't alone in her search. There were two of them to poke and ponder, two of them to put the pieces of the puzzle together, two of them to stop justice from being had.

That can't happen. They must be stopped! the voice insisted. Justice will be done!

Ironic that Ramona had picked Ryder to assist her... ironic that they would have to die together.

Chapter Nine

Following a restless night of more tossing and turning than sleeping, Willow headed for the saloon to meet Ryder, as promised.

The lights were off, the shutters were closed, and it took her eyes a moment to adjust to the gray gloom. He sat alone at the poker table, his lucky chips stacked neatly before him. Beneath his black brimmed hat, his expression was intent, his attention turned inward as though he was examining something deep inside himself. The way his long fingers continued to work automatically, shuffling and fanning the cards as expertly as any dealer, fascinated Willow.

Ryder fascinated her. He really was the fanciest man she'd ever known. Never in her life had she dreamed of being teamed up with a Sundance Kid look-alike—who dressed with more ruffles and embroidery than she ever had in her life—while simultaneously trying to find her sister and solve a murder.

And trying to avoid a romance.

Shaking herself free of the images that conjured, Willow made her way around several tables. "Ready?"

He jerked, his hand shooting toward his hip.

"Hey, I'm not armed!" she said, even as he froze.

"Shouldn't sneak up on a man like that," Ryder admonished.

"I wasn't sneaking. I was acting natural. You're just jumpy."

And the first thing he'd jumped for was his gun, reminding her of her first night in old Santa Fe, when he'd drawn the Colt .45 on Atchley.

Now, just as quick, he made the chips and cards disappear.

"Sure you're up to this?" he asked over the scrape of chair legs against wooden floor.

"What's Titus going to do to me in front of witnesses?"

Before retiring, they'd agreed the first stop would be the general store. Willow would go in, while Ryder waited out of sight. She was hoping that Velma would be alone, and that in the course of conversation, she'd get the woman to reveal the whereabouts of her husband when she'd been pushed into the kiva. If Titus hadn't been in the store that afternoon . . .

But they hadn't gotten halfway to the plaza when Ryder put a hand on her arm and pointed off to the right. Willow stopped to stare.

In the recess of a courtyard, Cal Atchley and Sheriff Landry were arguing in voices too low for them to hear what they were saying. His expression disgusted, Atchley dug into a pocket, pulled out a wad of money and shoved it at Landry. Without further comment, the cattleman whipped around and stalked inside the building. A grin splitting his beard-stubbled face, the sheriff stuck the bills in his pocket and came lumbering out of the courtyard.

Ryder challenged him. "Landry, how's the investigation on Ramona Cruz going?"

The large man was so surprised, he went slack-jawed. "Uh, got me some leads. My men are workin' on it."

"You wouldn't want to share what you know?"

"Couldn't do that with a citizen."

"Not even one with a real personal interest?" Ryder asked, hand smoothing over the ruffled front of his shirt to his throat, where the bruises were starting to fade.

"You'll be among the first to know when things get figured out."

Landry pushed past them and scurried away faster than Willow would have guessed he could move.

"Yeah, if we do the figuring," Ryder muttered.

Willow stared after the sheriff until he rounded a corner. "Do you think he's hiding something?"

"I think he's doing nothing. For one, Ramona was only a saloon girl, which doesn't exactly mean a whole lot to most people around here. For another, Atchley's evidently buying him off, as we just observed."

Making Willow wonder if it wasn't time for her to get to know Cal Atchley better—if he could overlook her interference in the hanging, that is. At the moment, however, she had other fish to fry.

When they neared the plaza, Willow and Ryder split up by design, he to a bench near the gazebo in the center of the square, she to the general store. She fought the instinct that bade her look back at him, just in case suspicious eyes were turned her way.

Inside the shop, Velma was focused on a short, stocky man wearing a dusty brown suit and bowler hat. No sign of Titus. Relieved, Willow entered.

The man was waving a bottle at the shopkeeper, and in a booming voice, proclaimed, "Brother Bart's Tonic is the finest elixir this side of the Mississippi. Feeling down? Not quite up to snuff? Got a fever coming on? No matter what's ailing you, I have a small miracle right here in my hand. Brother Bart's Tonic will fix you right up, good as new."

Willow noted the leather case on the floor and identified the man as a traveling salesman. Likewise, Velma noted her arrival.

"Willow, good morning!" she called.

"You're busy. Don't let me bother you."

"No bother," the salesman said, eyes widening. "Not when a pretty lady is involved. Barnabas Dunwoody, St. Louis, Missouri, at your service."

"Mr. Dunwoody." Willow inclined her head. "Willow Kane."

"Perhaps I can interest you in trying Brother Bart's Tonic, Miss Kane."

"Now, Mr. Dunwoody, that's not fair—trying to steal one of my customers, and right in my own store," Velma said, taking the sample from his hand. "I'll try a dozen bottles of your tonic. And if they sell, I'll take more next time you come through town."

The little man beamed. "Fair enough!"

They settled on a price, and Dunwoody dug bottles out of his case, while Velma removed cash from the register.

"Good doing business with you, Mrs. Whitiker."

Already creating a display on the counter, Velma waved him off. "See you next time, Mr. Dunwoody."

The salesman tipped his hat as he passed Willow and went whistling out the door.

Velma carried one of the bottles of tonic back to her sitting area and placed it on the shelf next to the belladonna canister. Willow noted the sundry herbs and teas, all marked, some sounding medicinal. Apparently, Velma tried various concoctions for herself. Willow wondered what ailed the shopkeeper. As usual, the potbellied stove was stoked despite the warm day, and Velma again wore a shawl.

Glancing at the display of tonic bottles that were no doubt filled with nothing more medicinal than alcohol with flavoring, Willow said, "I admire you, Velma. Running this store alone must be a challenge at times."

"Titus and I run it together."

"But you seem to be alone a lot."

"Often, Titus has errands to run," Velma said.

Making Willow want to ask if he'd run an *errand* the afternoon she'd gone out to the pueblo ruins. To Willow's dismay, even as she was trying to figure out how to manage it, Velma changed the subject.

"What can I do for you today, Willow?"

"Oh, I just wanted to apologize for yesterday." Maybe Velma would invite her to share that tea again, and she'd have the opportunity to steer the conversation back. "I had to run off so fast."

Exiting the back room, his sudden appearance making her jump, Titus growled, "And you can run again. Right back where you came from."

Damn! Willow's heart raced and her hopes sank. Now how was she going to find out what she came for?

"Titus, please," Velma said in that sweet, steel tone Willow recognized.

For once he ignored his wife. "You just jawing or are you buying?"

"I thought I'd look around some." Willow hoped that if she stalled, Titus would go away and give her another opportunity at Velma. "There are several things I need. It might take me a while."

But the man didn't budge. Willow began inspecting the wares on the counters and shelves and behind the glass display cases. Nervous under his thunderous gaze, she almost missed the bracelet. She'd moved past it before the significance registered.

"My God!" Willow whipped back around to the showy display case, a better look erasing any doubt. Silver and green turquoise. "Where did you get that bracelet?" she asked, pointing.

Titus answered. "What's it to you?"

"I gave this bracelet to my sister Tansy for her birthday."

"Oh, my!" Velma said.

"I didn't steal no one's pawn!" Titus informed her. "Traded it for some supplies."

"Tansy was here? You did business with her? Red hair, green eyes—"

Titus scowled even harder. "Didn't get it from no woman."

"Then who?"

"Wolf Madrid."

Willow was horrified. That mean-visaged, scary bounty hunter could only have gotten that bracelet from one source—Tansy herself. Undoubtedly he had been the man who'd given her the ride. Dear God, is that why she hadn't been able to find her sister? Because Madrid had Tansy stashed away in the ranch house? Tansy must have been in her glory when she first ran into the man.

Willow could only pray that her sister continued to hold the same opinion, that Madrid had done nothing awful to her...

"Oh, dear, you're white as a sheet." From behind the counter, Velma held out a bottle. "Perhaps one of Brother Bart's Tonics would help."

"No. Nothing." Realizing she was clutching on to the counter, Willow freed her grip. "Madrid with my sister. I only hope..."

"*Tch-tch-tch.* I understand your concern," Velma said, replacing the tonic in the display. "Well, you did want to know what happened to her. At least it's not as bad as what happened to my boy," she said, a sudden discordant note in her normally pleasant voice. "And the innocent shall suffer." Brow furrowing, Velma said, "You must save your sister, Willow, before it's too late. Madrid's living in a ranch house three quarters of the way to—"

"I know where he's living," Willow said, already heading for the door, her original purpose forgotten.

She raced across the street, straight toward a startled-looking Ryder. "C'mon," she urged, not stopping. "I know where Tansy is! We've got to get the horses."

Before going to the stable, Willow insisted on fetching her rifle. She wasn't going to face down Wolf Madrid unarmed. She remembered wanting to check the old ranch house when she'd been looking for Tansy and had given it up because she hadn't been willing to face Madrid with only a knife in hand.

Then someone had pushed her into the kiva...

Willow frowned, remembering. Wolf Madrid had been in the general store earlier when she'd asked after her sister. That must have been the very day he'd traded in Tansy's bracelet. And Willow remembered Madrid watching her ride out of town. Had *he* followed her and pushed her into the kiva? Not likely that both his and Titus's horses could have had loose shoes.

Too bad she couldn't have found out whether or not Titus was in the store that afternoon . . .

But at least she had a positive lead on Tansy, Willow told herself, that being more important than anything.

As they finally headed for the stable, Ryder asked, "So what's got you so all fired up? What makes you think you can find your sister now?"

"Tansy's silver-and-turquoise bracelet—I spotted it in one of the display cases."

"Pawn is a common item in these parts. How can you be sure this piece is hers?"

"Because I bought it for her." She turned her head and indicated the clasp holding her hair. "It matches this one."

Ryder nodded. "So she *has* been in town, probably right under our noses."

"Not exactly. Wolf Madrid brought the bracelet to the general store for trade."

"Madrid?"

His stiff tone told her Ryder wasn't liking the situation. No helping it, though. "I think he has her out at the old ranch house on Rancho Milagro property."

"You don't know that."

"Madrid is the best lead I've had so far."

Directly outside the stable, Ryder stopped short. "Going after Madrid isn't a good idea. The man's dangerous."

She set the butt of her rifle down. "All the more reason to get Tansy out of his clutches. Surely you're not about to suggest we let Sheriff Landry take care of it."

Ryder ignored that last comment, responding, "We need to think about this."

Willow realized Ryder wasn't just being contrary. He was tense. Afraid? Whatever the reason, he didn't want to face Madrid.

"There's nothing to think about." She lifted her rifle. "Stay here, if that's what you want. I'm going."

She started to turn away, but he gripped her upper arm. "You're not riding out alone to face Wolf Madrid."

Irritated by what sounded like a demand, she said, "You're not stopping me."

Ryder cursed under his breath, then said, "No, I'm going with you."

"Good."

Turning toward the barn, Willow came face-to-face with Miguel Borrego. How long had the stable owner been there? How much had he heard? And why did she care? She was about to be reunited with her sister, and that's all that mattered for the moment.

"We need our horses," Ryder told Borrego.

"Not going alone this time, I see," the stable owner said to Willow, his black gaze as spooky as the day she'd first brought Tequila in.

"No, this time I have protection."

"I'll go get your horses."

"We're in a hurry," she said, racing by him. "We'll see to them ourselves."

Willow could feel Borrego's stare follow her into the gloom of the barn. Ryder didn't say anything, just followed her lead. Still not trusting Borrego, she felt safer seeing to Tequila herself. And getting their own horses was quicker—no more time for arguments.

They rode out in near silence and kept up a fast pace that didn't allow for chatting. Willow took the lead. Halfway to the ranch house, Ryder drew up alongside her.

"I guess now you'll be heading home." Then he clarified, "To the twentieth century."

"We haven't found Tansy yet."

"If we do."

"I guess," she agreed.

Willow didn't want to think that far ahead. Didn't want to consider never seeing Ryder again and how that would make her feel. For his help in rescuing her sister, she would be grateful to him always. Thinking beyond that brought a lump to her throat, and a funny feeling in her chest, so she concentrated on other things instead.

Like how they were going to get Tansy away from Wolf Madrid without trouble, a seemingly impossible situation.

RYDER COULDN'T BELIEVE he was riding right into the bounty hunter's den. He needed to have *his* head examined. He might as well stick it through another noose. He knew it would only have been a matter of time before Madrid came gunning for him, anyway. At least this way he had the advantage.

Then, again, maybe Madrid didn't know. Maybe no one was after him, and he'd finally left his past behind. Ryder hoped so. He'd been looking over his shoulder, waiting for the past to catch up with him, for far too long.

The dead did haunt a man, though, one way or another.

The living could haunt a man, too. Like Willow. Though she rode before him, in spirit she was already gone to her own time. With each mile, Ryder felt the distance grow, felt her slip further and further away, out of his reach. For years he'd been empty, a shell of a man with nothing inside. Willow had changed that. Somehow, she had filled him. With her spirit. With her caring. With her courage.

He didn't know how he was going to let her go.

He had to let go, Ryder told himself. Better for her. Safer. This wasn't a matter of what he wanted.

They rode through and out of a valley. Ahead lay Mesa Milagro, the stark planes of striated rock burnished by the midday sun.

High noon. An appropriate time for a showdown, Ryder thought wryly, as a small ranch house came into sight.

Willow slowed her horse. "There it is." She stood in her stirrups and squinted at the place. "I don't see any horse in the corral."

Ryder followed the direction of her gaze. "Me, neither."

"Then getting Tansy away will be a piece of cake!" she said, digging her heels into Tequila's sides.

Ryder kept up with her, his attention shifting in every direction. If danger were to come at them, he didn't want to be surprised. But search as he might, the only movement he saw was a hawk wheeling on a breeze.

In front of the house, they dismounted, Willow racing to the front door, throwing it open and yelling, "Tansy!"

No response from within. A sense of foreboding that had nothing to do with danger filled Ryder as he followed and stepped through the doorway. A quick look around assured him the room was empty but for a few pieces of furniture. A table and two chairs on one side of the fireplace. A wood-and-leather sofa and rocking chair flanking the other side. Willow disappeared into the other room.

"Tansy!" came a plaintive cry that tore at Ryder's heart. "Where are you?" Then she stepped back into the main room, her luminous brown eyes filling with tears. "She's not here anymore, Ryder! And neither are Madrid's clothes. He's gone. Where could he have taken Tansy?"

"You don't even know for certain that your sister was here."

"She had to be!" Like a cougar, Willow stalked the length of the room. She checked every shelf, looked into every corner. "Someone gave her a ride away from the pueblo ruins. And Madrid brought her bracelet to the general store, so it must have been him." She took a deep breath. "If he hurt her, I'll find the bastard and shoot him dead!"

The short hairs on Ryder's neck stood straight. "You won't have to. I'll do it for you." One more mark against his soul wouldn't matter, but she was an innocent.

Willow didn't answer, and Ryder realized she'd stopped pacing. Near the fireplace, she was standing very still. Her gaze was focused. Then she reached toward the seat of the rocker and picked up whatever held her fascinated.

"This is hers. She cut her English class to buy it." She turned and held out the proof. "Tansy *was* here, Ryder!"

One look at the evidence in her hand froze him to the spot.

CLOSE. SO VERY CLOSE. Willow imagined she could still feel the warmth of her sister's fingers as she turned the pages of *McCreery and the Quick-draw Kid* and read by the firelight. But Tansy was gone. Out of her reach once more. As if fate were determined to keep the sisters separated forever. She pressed the dime novel to her breast and realized tears slipped from her eyes and down her cheeks.

"What if I never see her again?"

"You'll see her again," Ryder said, his tone sympathetic. "Don't give up. This is the closest we've gotten. Next time we'll find her."

But Willow couldn't be consoled. The signs of Madrid's departure were obvious. Clothes gone. No supplies on the shelves. No wood stacked by the fireplace. And hadn't there been two horses in the corral the first night she'd seen him? The corral was as empty as she felt at that moment.

And then Ryder took her in his arms and some of the emptiness filled with him. She let go, her sobs muffled against his shoulder. He stroked her hair, her neck, the small of her back. She pressed into him, wanting comfort, wanting oblivion from the pain she was feeling.

Lifting her head, she curled her fingers around his neck and locked gazes with him. Tried losing herself in those beautiful blue eyes. Wet her lips, a prelude to his kiss.

Ryder didn't disappoint her. He took her mouth while murmuring her name and crushing her to him.

His kiss took her breath away, but it couldn't make her mind go blank. Couldn't chase away the image she had of Tansy showing her the dime novel, of Tansy growing furious when Willow grounded her. Her sister might have slipped into the past by accident, but what if she made good on her threat? What if she didn't want to be found, didn't want to go home?

Her anguish filtered into the kiss.

And Ryder let go of her.

"Don't stop," she begged.

"This isn't the right time, Willow. It's not me you're thinking of."

"Who cares—"

"I do."

Ashamed, Willow realized how wrong she'd been to use Ryder merely to ease her pain. He deserved more. And so did she. "I'm sorry."

"Don't be. I understand."

Gazing into his eyes, she believed him. She read loss there, and sorrow—things she hadn't noticed before. Had he hidden them from her? Or had she just been too blind, too focused on her own needs to recognize his?

"You *do* understand, don't you?"

He nodded and thumbed the path of her tears along the hollow of her cheek. "I lost my whole family and nothing's going to bring *them* back."

"Lost them how?"

"They're all dead." With a faraway, sad look in his eyes, he quickly turned away. "Let's get back to town."

Willow tucked the dime novel into a vest pocket and left the house that had sheltered her sister at least for a few days. "Maybe we can track Madrid and Tansy."

A futile effort, for Madrid had obviously been in and out of the corral too many times for them to determine which set to follow, Willow realized. None of the prints stood out as being newer than the others. And if two riders had gone out together, they couldn't tell. What they needed was a professional tracker to sort all the prints out. So, her spirits down, they set off for Santa Fe, letting the horses set their own pace.

As she rode, Willow gave herself a pep talk. Tansy would be all right. Just because she was with Wolf Madrid didn't mean he'd hurt her. Or used her sexually—another concern of Willow's, especially considering how crazy her sister had been about the hero of those books. For all she knew, Willow told herself, Tansy was safe and having the time of her life.

She had to believe that or go out of her mind with worry.

Knowing Ryder was worried, too, made her feel better. She realized how much she'd come to count on his support in just a few days. And how she was counting on a man she knew virtually nothing about. That his family was dead was the first thing he'd revealed about himself. After having his strong shoulder to cry on about Tansy, Willow couldn't let the admission go without commiserating.

She drew Tequila even with Gold Rush and said, "I'm sorry about your family."

Ryder stiffened in the saddle but didn't respond.

Determined to know more, she didn't give up. "You said they were dead. How?"

"Slaughtered."

"By Indians?"

His jaw hardened. "By white men's bullets."

He dug his heels into the palomino's sides, and the horse moved faster. Willow followed, accepting the fact that Ryder wasn't going to say more. Not now. Maybe never.

And what did it matter? She'd be returning to her own time, even though the when of it escaped her. She might be on her way now if Tansy had been in the house. How much longer could she wait to find her sister? How much more disappointment could she take?

As much as it took to find Tansy, Willow told herself grimly, for she wasn't about to make another trip through time alone.

"BORREGO, WHERE ARE YOU?" Ryder called when they dismounted at the stable.

No answer.

"Maybe he's off tying one on again...uh, getting drunk," Willow clarified.

"I could see if he's home." He indicated the shack at the back of the corral.

"I'm not that tired. Why don't we just see to the horses ourselves."

Willow didn't mind. All she had to look forward to was another night of serving drinks at the saloon. She'd run out of ideas and was feeling discouraged.

"Let's go," Ryder agreed, leading the way back toward their stalls.

The horses were restless, moving around and snorting, making Willow wonder if Borrego had fed and watered them yet. They'd have to find the man before going to supper. If they were capable of finding anyone...

Not wanting her mind to wander into dangerous territory, she concentrated on relieving Tequila of his tack. She'd barely gotten the cinch on his saddle loose when she heard a noise like metal striking a hard surface coming from the rear of the building. She craned her neck and stared toward the back, but saw nothing to alarm her in the inky recesses of the barn. The sound must have been closer than she'd imagined—undoubtedly one of the horses.

She finished undoing the cinch, removed the saddle and blanket and set them on a rail outside the stall. A horse whinnied and another banged against a wall. What was going on? Willow was removing Tequila's bridle and bit when she swore she heard a door clicking closed. Hanging the bridle on a peg next to the saddle, she stopped to listen.

The horses were getting more restless. In several stalls, hooves contacted boards. One horse made a funny blowing sound through his nose and another neighed.

"What's going on?" Ryder called to her.

"I don't know." Then a distinct sharp scent assaulted her, and her blood stilled. "Oh, no, do you smell it?"

"What?"

"Smoke! Back there somewhere."

Ryder caught up with her as she rushed to find its source. Fire in a barn could spell disaster. Old wood. Dry hay. So much tinder...so many horses...

The smell got stronger. Suddenly, from a pile of straw, flames shot up before them, blocking the rear exit. Ryder grabbed Willow and pulled her back, away from the blaze.

"Oh, my God! How are we going to put it out?"

"Two of us? We can't. We gotta get help."

Even as they ran back through the building, horses squealed in fright. Willow was frightened, too, and thought about letting Ryder go for help while she pulled horses out of their stalls. She couldn't abandon them. Then she realized the entrance doors were shut. Ryder must have realized it, too, for he cursed and ran faster, ramming his shoulder against the wooden panel.

It didn't budge—someone had locked them in.

They were trapped in a burning barn!

Chapter Ten

Ryder jammed his shoulder into the double doors again, but they didn't budge. This was no accident. To his everlasting horror, someone had set a fire and locked them inside the barn with every intention of burning them to death.

Willow. He couldn't let another person he cared for die!

"Look around for a tool of some kind," he said, not that they could see much with the doors closed. Only a single window high up and too small for an adult to crawl through gave them any light. "There's gotta be a shovel or pitchfork around here. Maybe we can break through the wood."

"Hurry! The fire's spreading!"

Indeed, the rear wall caught fire and flared. Ryder's gut tightened and he tried to block out the squeals of the terrified animals surrounding them. Had justice finally caught up to him? How unfair that Willow and more than a dozen horses would burn, as well.

"You take that side," Ryder said, going opposite.

They spent the next few minutes searching every corner, every stall, as smoke rolled down the aisle and became trapped over their heads by the low roof. Ryder's eyes stung and his lungs began to hurt with every breath. He pulled his bandanna up, covering his nose and mouth, even as a frantic horse reared and crushed Ryder between his massive body and the wall. The air squeezed out of his lungs, but he somehow maneuvered the animal aside and slipped back out of the stall.

"I found the pitchfork!" Willow shouted, her words punctuated by a harsh cough.

"Good work."

Cutting through the thickening smoke, Ryder was at Willow's side in a minute. She was just pulling up her bandanna as he had. He took the tool and dragged her away from the blaze that was consuming the rear wall.

"The horses," she said, her muffled words punctuated by a pounding of hooves.

Ryder glanced back at the stalls nearest the fire. One of the horses had broken loose and was wheeling in the aisle, his dark body outlined by golden flames.

"I'll get him!"

Willow slipped from his grasp and ran toward the panicked animal. Unable to stop her, Ryder turned his attention to getting them all out. But the first time he drove the pitchfork into the doors, he knew the task wouldn't be easy. The wood was thick and sturdy. He could ram until his arms were sore, but he'd probably expire from lack of air before getting through.

Air! He crashed the pitchfork through the tiny window to buy them some time. A loud crack and a rushing sound behind him made him whirl around. Willow was leading the prancing horse toward him.

Beyond her, part of the roof caved in with a rain of dirt.

"Stay here!" he demanded. He figured the ceiling was only made up of sod probably less than a foot thick laid in over wooden beams. "I'm going to try to go up through the roof!"

Nearby, he found a wooden chair and positioned it directly next to a stall. Then he climbed onto the seat and tested the ceiling with the pitchfork. Relief poured through him when the metal prongs easily sliced into the sod. But below, Willow ignored his demand. After leaving the horse loose at the front of the barn, she raced back to get another. Ryder was certain she would continue until she dropped.

Twisting the pitchfork, he prayed he'd be able to get himself out and open the doors before that happened. Dry earth sifted down into his face. He pulled the tool out and plunged it into the sod again, a few inches away from the first entry. He repeated the twisting motion and was rewarded with a clump of earth plopping on his chest.

Plunge... twist... plunge... twist.

Earth and dried grass began raining down on him until he saw daylight through a ragged hole. "Got it!"

Willow was shooing two horses toward the front of the barn. "Thank God."

Even as she ran back, he assessed the situation. The fire was creeping overhead. He worked faster, harder, and soon had a hole big enough to pass through.

"I'm going to try to get out!" he shouted above equine squeals as another horse flew toward the loose ones.

That he got no response from Willow worried him, but he couldn't stop now. Finding footing at the top of the stall, he used it to launch himself up and through the hole, levering his hands on the outside of the roof. The sod sank under his weight, but it didn't give, because he was balanced over a *viga*, a solid wooden beam. The muscles of his arms burned as he dragged himself out of the barn and onto the roof. Collapsing, he tore the bandanna from his face and gulped in air.

Then he crawled to the edge of the roof. Below, people on the street passed by, seemingly unaware of the drama being played out a dozen yards from their path. Using another *viga*, which jutted nearly two feet from the side of the building, Ryder swung his body over the edge, got his bearings and dropped to the ground.

Before him, a small boy tugged at his mother's skirts. "Mama, look at that man."

The woman turned, eyes widening as they went beyond Ryder and focused. "Fire! Fire! Fire!" She screamed and screamed, her voice shrill over the cries of her child.

Immediately, the street was swarming with other people calling out for help. Ryder removed the plank of wood that had held him and Willow prisoner, then threw the barn doors wide open.

Huge clouds of smoke billowed out of the building, and a half-dozen loose horses charged him.

Jumping out of the way, he yelled, "Willow!" No answer. "I'm coming to get you! Hold on!"

"Hey, you can't go back in there," someone said.

Turning from the smoke, Ryder tried to get some fresh air. "The hell I can't. There's a woman in there." He pulled up the bandanna. "And more horses."

Ryder ignored the mutterings of help coming and plunged through the smoke-filled interior, aware that a couple of other people followed and were opening the front stalls to release the remaining horses.

"Willow?" he called. "If you can hear me, answer."

He was moving down the aisle blind now, though every so often new wood would torch, casting an eerie, dancing light over the smoky interior. The rear stalls were engulfed in flames. The horses that had been stabled there would have been burned alive if not for Willow.

But where was she?

"Willow!" he shouted at the top of his lungs.

To no avail.

Ryder had gone as far as he dared. Heat seared him from every direction. Flames sucked at dry wood that moaned and popped and surrendered with a sigh. He stood in the belly of the inferno—a living, breathing entity—and feared he'd lost the woman who'd given him back some of his humanity.

Something inside Ryder died.

The blaze edged closer, sparks reaching out to caress him, and Ryder told himself to leave, to save himself. But he couldn't force his legs to move. Couldn't make the effort. Not without her.

He stood frozen, heart encased in ice, until he heard a cough somewhere behind and to his right.

"Willow?" His heart thundered. It had to be her.

His legs moved then, turning him, taking him farther away from the flames, moving from one stall to the next until he found her. She was struggling to raise herself from the ground and coughing some more.

The fire hadn't won, after all.

Ryder lifted her to her feet and then into his arms. Her head lolled against his neck, and her coughs came in fits and starts as he rushed her out to the street and into the path of a bucket of water. Townspeople and soldiers alike had formed a fire brigade and were doing what they could to contain the flames. Ryder removed his bandanna, then hers.

Coming fully awake, Willow was pushing at him. "Let me down. I can walk," she insisted between coughs.

"Sure you can. You can do anything when you set your mind to it. Even save a bunch of horses."

"They got out okay?"

"They got out."

Willow stopped struggling. Then as Ryder escaped the melee and looked for a place to set her down, Miguel Borrego popped out of nowhere, looking properly horrified and blocking their exit.

"My barn!" He began cursing in Spanish. "What have you done to my barn?"

"More like what your barn almost did to us. Convenient of you to show up now," Ryder said coldly.

"I was not gone so long." Borrego's eyes were wide, shifting between the scene of destruction and Ryder.

"Just long enough that we almost burned to death," Willow said, voice hoarse.

"You are not blaming me? You think I would do this to my own business? For what reason?"

"The same reason three men tried to hang me." Who would want vengeance for Ramona's death more than the man who'd loved her? "Now get outa my way."

Ryder stepped around him, and a woman guided them to the other side of the street, away from the smoke and confusion. "You can bring her in here." The woman indicated a courtyard behind an adobe wall. "I'll get a doctor."

"And the sheriff," Ryder said, though he didn't know what good Landry would do if he showed.

The woman nodded and hurried off.

Ryder crossed the courtyard to a bench where he set Willow down. A handful of people followed and milled around, asking questions about how the fire started.

"That's an answer the sheriff needs to find," Ryder said, steadying Willow through another coughing spell.

"Are you saying someone set the fire on purpose?" asked a short man wearing a suit and making notes with a stubby pencil.

Figuring him to be a newspaperman, Ryder nodded. "That's what I'm saying. And that someone locked us inside."

A collective gasp went through the small crowd. Ryder looked around, tried to determine if an arsonist stood among them. Some faces he recognized, some he didn't. All the faces were openly shocked, except the one belonging to a breed who stood back from the crowd, watching with a closed expression. Something about the man...

Then Willow's coughing grabbed his whole attention.

"Let the lady have some air," a woman said.

Grumbling, the bystanders backed off.

"You all right?" Ryder asked Willow.

Covered with soot and coughing up more, she was still the most welcome sight he'd ever seen. She grinned at him, her teeth white against her grimy face, and his chest squeezed tight again, but this time it was a good feeling.

"You're one up on me," she said, her voice hoarse. "So I owe you one."

"Owe me one what?"

"Rescue. I might have saved your hide to begin with, but this is the second time you've saved mine."

Making Ryder wonder if he had been the sole target in the barn as he'd assumed. The relief he'd been feeling was replaced by worry. And by the certainty that the only thing that would keep Willow safe would be to find Tansy quick and send the sisters back where they belonged.

"THE FIRE WAS NO ACCIDENT. The barn doors didn't get locked by accident!" Ryder shouted in Sheriff Landry's face a while later.

Willow put a hand on his arm. She didn't know why he'd insisted on a face-off with the sheriff, anyway. A lot of good it would do them. The doctor had checked her over. Except for a tight, sore feeling in her chest and an occasional cough, she was fine.

"I'll put some men on it," Landry promised.

"While you're at it, get some men to find this lady's kid sister. Her name's Tansy Kane. She's got bright red hair and green eyes. And Wolf Madrid's got her."

"Madrid?" the sheriff echoed.

Willow would swear he went pale. "We were out by his place today looking for her. Only the house was empty. He took off with her."

"So what do you expect me to do?"

"Track the bastard down and get Willow's sister back!" Ryder's eyes were glittering as he gave the sheriff a look of contempt.

Sweat trickled from Landry's forehead. "I don't know of any trackers around right now. Maybe someone at the fort can help you."

"I can do it."

A man stepped out of the crowd. The same man Willow had noticed after leaving the sheriff's office—the half Indian wearing white man's clothes and moccasins. Again she had the impression that he was vaguely familiar.

"You a tracker?" Ryder asked, his voice ripe with suspicion. "How much experience?"

The man didn't take his dark eyes off Willow. "Enough."

Landry cleared his throat. "I don't know—"

Ryder cut him off. "Doesn't surprise me. How much do you want?"

"We can settle that later." The man turned to go. "If I find the lady's sister."

"Wait a minute," Willow protested. "You don't even know where to start."

"I know," he said, slipping through the crowd.

Only after he'd disappeared did Willow realize she didn't know the man's name or where to find him, nor did he know those things about her. Then she figured if he could find Tansy, he certainly could track her down.

"Can we get out of here now?" she asked Ryder.

She couldn't wait to get back to her room and feel water and soap slide over her skin. Soot-covered and smelling like smoke, she would come clean. She only hoped her clothes were salvageable.

"Can you walk?"

"Of course I can walk." Then she started. "Oh, Tequila. What happened to the horses?"

"Some of them soldiers rounded 'em up, ma'am," a grizzled old-timer volunteered. "They was gonna find a corral somewhere. Don't worry, soldiers know how to take proper care of their animals."

"I'm sure they do," she said, though she wanted to find hers and make certain straight off.

Undoubtedly able to read her mind, Ryder assured her, "I'll find Tequila and Gold Rush after I get you back to your room."

Willow didn't have the energy to fight. "All right." She allowed him to lead her through the people still gathered in the courtyard. "While you're at it, think you can scare up some tack? And my rifle's gone," she complained, coughing.

Though once she set foot on the street, Willow felt eternally grateful when she saw what was left of Borrego's Stable—charcoal rubble and a debris-littered corral.

"We could have died in there," she whispered, shivering.

Ryder pulled her closer. "But we didn't," he replied and covered her mouth with his, the action life-affirming.

Her emotions at fever pitch, Willow clung to Ryder as if he were her lifeline. And he was. He'd saved her life. That meant something. That they were destined to be together. But how? The question dizzied Willow as he released her and led her off to the hotel.

Thank God they'd come through the ordeal whole. As for the stable owner...it looked like the man would have to rely on his guitar playing to make a living, at least until he could do something about rebuilding his business.

Or until they could prove Miguel Borrego set fire to his own barn to kill them.

"WHAT AN ORDEAL you must have been through," Ottilie said, her French accent making *ordeal* sound romantic.

The women who worked the saloon all sat in the kitchen eating supper together. As usual, they surrounded an old scarred plank table, passing dishes. The Mexican cook hovered in the background after having made certain that Willow had a pitcher of lemonade all for herself—to help her throat, he'd said.

"I would have been too terrified to move," Amabelle pronounced.

Rosabelle added, "And you saved all those horses."

"She's a regular heroine," Benita said dryly.

Hazel gave the Mexican woman a chastising glare. "Say it like you mean it, honey. When did you ever do something so brave?"

"You might be surprised at what I've done."

Though her tone was cold, Benita sounded as if she was bragging. Willow shifted uneasily, then assured herself the Mexican woman merely wanted to be the center of attention no matter the situation.

"You're making too much fuss, anyway," she told them all.

Though the food held little interest for Willow, she forced herself to eat a bit of everything, taking sips of lemonade between bites. She had to keep her strength up, but how was she supposed to have an appetite considering the circumstances? She did a good enough job of fooling everyone into thinking she was all right when really she wasn't. She even managed a smile when she excused herself from the table.

Back in her room, she inspected herself for any signs of the fire, any reminder of the terror she'd lived through. Before going down to supper, she'd scrubbed every inch of skin and had washed her hair three times. Still, the smell of the fire wouldn't leave her. Nor the taste, sight, sound. The memory permeated her senses.

Someone had tried to kill her.

Willow pushed away the spooky knowledge. Time to get ready for work.

A dress of festive red satin appealed to her tonight. The skirts were full, the top cut low, though not immodestly so. The swell of her breasts barely peeked over the bodice. Then she French braided her masses of hair, fastening Tansy's clasp at her neck and letting the tail hang free down her back. Her skirts not only jingled as she left the room, but the material rustled, as well.

Work helped Willow forget the horror of the fire, although she wasn't moving too fast. Her energy was drained, no doubt because her lungs felt as if they were wrapped in cotton.

Halfway through the night, she realized Ryder hadn't showed. As a matter of fact, the poker table was sparsely attended. Titus Whitiker was nowhere to be seen, and Cal Atchley sat in a corner drinking alone.

She'd been thinking she needed to get to know the cattleman better, so Willow approached his table as though she didn't doubt he'd be happy to talk to her. He was too busy pouring himself a shot glass of whiskey to notice. She stopped before the vacant chair at his table and waited while Atchley threw the liquor to the back of his throat in one smooth motion.

"I'm taken care of," he said, slamming the whiskey glass down on the table.

"But you don't have company."

His gray eyes bored into her. "Why would I want yours?"

"Why wouldn't you?"

Atchley barked a laugh and poured another drink. "Sit if you must," he growled.

Willow slid into the chair, aware that he was still staring at her. "Like what you see?"

"Spooky. You don't *really* look like her, but if I had a few more of these . . . I might be able to make myself believe she was still alive."

"Ramona."

"Ramona," he echoed.

"Sounds like you had a thing for her."

"She was that kind of woman. *You* that kind of woman?"

"I doubt it."

"Mmm." He pulled a face. "You're the kind of woman who goes around freeing murderers."

"You don't know that Ryder did it."

"You don't know he didn't."

Willow ignored the truth of his words. "He thinks you may be the one."

"So he says. Talks a good game whether he's playing poker or . . . whatever."

"You'd accuse a man of murder simply because the victim was found holding one of his lucky chips?" Supposedly, Atchley had found the memento . . . or had he pretended to? she wondered.

"The victim was afraid of him."

Willow started. She hadn't heard this before. "Afraid?" Not that she couldn't believe it. Ryder had his dark moments, all right. "Why?"

"Don't know exactly. Said he was dangerous and she had proof."

"What kind of proof?"

"Didn't say."

"Maybe she was just talking."

Atchley shook his head. "Don't think so. A man knows when a woman has reason to be afraid." His voice was gruff. "He can see it in her eyes."

"A man would have to be pretty close to a woman to see that, though. Were you close to Ramona, Mr. Atchley?"

"Close enough!"

His vehemence startled Willow. Ryder indicated Atchley's jealousy might have led the rancher to kill her and place the blame elsewhere. But somehow, Willow didn't sense in him the kind of evil it would take to kill someone he loved. He was the kind of man who bought a house in town for his sickly wife, for heaven's sake.

But those he hated were another story.

No matter that he'd denied it, she was certain Cal Atchley had sent his boys after Ryder to string him up. Had he told them to finish the job earlier today? Or maybe he'd torched the barn himself.

Even as the rancher swallowed another shot, Willow was distracted. She sensed eyes boring into the middle of her back. Expecting to find Ryder staring at her, she turned in her chair, confused for a moment when she didn't see her fancy man. Then she spotted the tracker across the room. He was standing in the shadows near the stairs that led to the rooms above.

His dark unreadable gaze connected with hers and drew her out of her chair.

Heart racing, she said, "You'll have to excuse me."

Please let him have found Tansy.

"Sit. It was just gettin' interesting."

"Another time, perhaps," she promised.

Atchley cursed and mumbled, "Suit yourself."

Willow was already cutting across the saloon's floor, dodging tables, her focus the man who could tell her about her sister.

Again struck by a familiarity she couldn't explain, she tried to place him. She felt as if she'd seen that harsh, yet attractively exotic face before, but she didn't know where or when. And it wasn't just his features that seemed familiar. It was a feeling...an instinct...a certainty....

As she drew closer and his expression remained closed, Willow's stomach knotted with certainty of another kind. She stopped directly in front of the man, heart in her throat.

"You didn't find her, did you?"

"The tracks were too old."

"What are you talking about? They're a day at the most."

"Madrid's latest tracks *are* no more than a day old," he agreed. "But he was alone."

"That's impossible. Tansy was there. I found her book! And he had two horses."

He nodded. "But two horses didn't go out together, not yesterday. I followed other tracks a ways. One set plain faded out. The others I lost in a rocky area. Sorry I can't tell you more."

Willow was devastated. She hadn't realized how much she'd been counting on the stranger's finding some solid lead on her sister. Could no one locate a bright, fairly obtrusive fifteen-year-old?

"Madrid will come back," he said. "Always does."

Mouth and throat as dry as they had been directly after the fire, she croaked, "What do I owe you?"

"Nothing." Features drawn into an expression of sympathy and something more, something deeper, he added, "I didn't find what you were looking for."

A lump growing in her throat, she nodded and edged toward the stairs. "Thank you for trying."

Willow thought he was about to say something else, and she saw what appeared to be a great wave of sadness wash over him. Oddly enough, she found herself wanting to comfort him. That was ridiculous, of course. He had no reason to be sad, and she was the one who needed comforting.

Then he turned away, his retreat silent. Willow started up the stairs. Only when she hit the landing did she realize she didn't even know the tracker's name. Meaning to fix that, she leaned over the rail. Too late. Once more, he'd vanished.

Tears started before she got the door to her room open. Inside, Willow threw herself across the bed, vaguely registering a crinkling sound as her skirts slid across the coverlet. Griefstricken, now truly believing that she might never see Tansy again, she couldn't stop the tears from flowing. She wasn't a woman who cried often—she'd wept more in the past few days than she had in the whole of her adult years—and the tears embarrassed her.

Hell, she deserved a good cry!

Giving in to emotion, Willow wept until her tear ducts were exhausted and her eyes were swollen. She lay there in the dark for some time afterward, knowing she wasn't going to go back downstairs. Not to-night. Tonight she was in mourning. Hazel would understand. Besides, she was exhausted from the fire. Perhaps sunlight would bring with it a renewed hope. She wanted to believe that.

Eventually, when she didn't even approach sleep, Willow grew tired of the dark. Sliding off the bed to do something about it, she heard the strange crin-kling sound again. Like paper rather than material. After lighting the lamp on her dresser, she investi-gated, lifting her skirts and the coin-laden lacy petti-coats attached to her dress. Between the layers, at hip level, she found what looked like an envelope.

"Ramona, you pack rat," she murmured. "What now?"

She ripped the sewn edge free from the material and quickly opened the envelope. A folded piece of yel-lowed paper lay inside. Hands trembling, she re-moved the missive from its nest and smoothed it out.

The sketch of a man with pale hair and a dark mus-tache staring back at Willow gave her a start. Her fin-gers crushed the edges of the paper as she read:

WANTED
Ryder McCreery
for the terrible murder of
Pete Kavanaugh
May his soul Rest in Peace
REWARD—$1,000.
Contact Kansas City Pinkerton Office

Willow's stomach knotted. Ryder McCreery. Ry-der Smith? How many Ryders with pale hair and dark mustaches could there possibly be?

And how many people had bad opinions of Ryder or had gone so far as to warn her about him?

Cal Atchley and his vigilantes... Titus and Velma... Farley and Benita.

Why hadn't she listened?

And why had Ramona hidden the flyer in her petticoats? Had she been blackmailing Ryder, threatening to turn him in? Is that why she was afraid of him? Is that why she had died?

Willow didn't want to believe it, didn't want to believe Ryder was a killer. But the Wanted flyer proclaimed that he was one. She stared at the paper in her hands, as if it could tell her the truth about the man she'd come to care about, the man she'd come to depend on.

Ryder McCreery.

She'd heard the name before.

Tansy's book. The reason her sister had skipped English class. The thing that had started this whole tragic adventure.

McCreery and the Quick-draw Kid.

Willow pulled the slim tome from the drawer where she'd stuffed it. The man sketched in the foreground was mostly turned away from the viewer, but enough of him could be seen to know he had pale hair and a dark mustache. She sank into a chair and turned up the light.

Opening the dime novel that had taken her sister from her, Willow began to read.

COULD NO ONE DIE like they were supposed to?

Both of them getting out of the stable alive—this must be some kind of curse!

But curses were meant to be broken, weren't they?

Especially if one had the right leverage. Admittedly, that had been missing before. But not anymore. Ironic how things worked out.

It was a sign.

Using that leverage judiciously would ensure Ryder and Ramona got exactly what they deserved.

Chapter Eleven

Early the next morning, Willow dressed in clothes that still smelled faintly of smoke even after being washed. She strapped on her knife and dug into her saddlebags. Among other things, she'd thrown her keys inside. Attached to the key ring was a canister of pepper gas that she removed and pocketed. Having lost her rifle in the fire, she could use any weapon she could get.

Ready as she was going to be, and not wanting to alert Ryder, Willow sneaked out of her room and down the stairs. Hopefully she wouldn't have too much trouble finding where Ryder had stabled Tequila. After all she'd learned about the man, she didn't trust him to tell her the truth about anything, so she'd figure it out for herself. When Ryder had tapped at her door the night before, she hadn't answered, had let him think she was sleeping. The way she was feeling, she didn't want to face him at all. And maybe she wouldn't have to.

Willow swallowed her disappointment at the way things had turned out between them—not that they'd had any kind of future together, anyway, she reminded herself—and put her mind to her plan for the day.

Before leaving the building, she entered the saloon and found the shotgun Hazel kept under the bar. She broke open the weapon and noted both chambers were filled. Then she removed several cartridges from the box of ammunition and stuck them in her vest pockets. She was certain the saloon owner wouldn't mind her borrowing the weapon for a good cause.

Willow wasn't about to face Wolf Madrid unarmed.

She left the saloon and headed in the opposite direction from the plaza, to another stable down the street, Santa Fe Livery.

As she'd hoped, the first light of dawn had filled her with a new determination. The tracker had said Madrid always came back. That's what she was counting on. She would head for the old ranch house and wait for the bounty hunter to return. She'd force him to tell her what he'd done with Tansy. If he didn't show today, she'd try again tomorrow. And the next day and as many days after that as necessary!

Outside the fancy Santa Fe Livery, a stable hand was tightening the cinch on a horse for a customer, who slipped money into his hand and rode off.

Willow approached the worker, whose fair hair was slicked back from a young face. "Excuse me, but do you have any of the horses from Borrego's Stable here?"

He gave her a once-over that told her he wasn't as young as he looked. "Sure do. Which one you lookin' for?"

"Name's Tequila. An Appaloosa. A man named Ryder Smith would have brought him in with his palomino, Gold Rush."

"I wasn't here late yesterday. Let me check." The young man disappeared into the barn, and a moment later called out. "I think this is him, miss. Come look."

To Willow's relief, he had found Tequila. She quickly checked over the gelding to make certain he had no injuries from the fire.

"He seems sound."

"You wanna take him out?"

"That's why I'm here. Only I lost my tack in the fire. Can I rent some?"

The stable hand checked a nearby wall holding saddles and blankets, bits and bridles. The pegs were numbered as were the stalls. "Looks like your friend replaced what you lost." He removed the bit and bridle from its peg. "Give me a few minutes and I'll fix you right up."

A half hour later, Willow was well on her way to Rancho Milagro. She tried not to think about Ryder's motives in taking care of Tequila for her. All she could think of was the Wanted flyer and the dime novel. According to *McCreery and the Quick-draw Kid*, Ryder had killed several men in a shoot-out before he'd met up with Pete "Quick-draw" Kavanaugh. The novel romanticized the whole thing, of course. Dramatically, it told how the Quick-draw Kid had *forced* Ryder to engage in a showdown.

Willow reminded herself that any novel was fiction, that dime novels in particular greatly exaggerated the real-life exploits of their heroes. All she knew was that according to the story, Ryder had killed some men, and although she couldn't be certain if it was true, she had to consider the possibility.

Therefore, she could no longer fully trust him.

As always, Willow had no one to depend on but herself. She'd forgotten that for a while. She'd fallen under Ryder's spell. But the spell was broken.

As was her heart.

Shoving the disturbing thought aside, ignoring the sadness that welled up and threatened to choke her, Willow realized she was almost at her destination. She guided Tequila up a grassy knoll from the top of which she could see the ranch house. To her surprise, smoke rolled out of the chimney. And a black horse grazed in the corral. Her pulse buzzed through her at the unexpected circumstances.

Wolf Madrid had already returned!

Thrown for a moment, Willow decided directness was in order. Not enough growth around the place to hide her approach. She'd have to ride straight up to his door and give Madrid a real special *how-de-do* when he opened it. She slipped the shotgun from its sheath and snugged it next to her leg. In case he heard Tequila and looked out a window, she didn't want Madrid to see that she was armed and ready for him.

But if he noted her arrival, the bounty hunter didn't rush out to greet her. Directly in front of the house, Willow slipped off Tequila, carefully sliding the shotgun close to the saddle. She banged on the door and prepared herself.

Everything inside was still, and so she was startled when the door was suddenly thrown open. Shoulder-length hair loose around his mean-looking face, Madrid stood there scowling down at her. Regaining her composure with difficulty, Willow lifted the shotgun and, taking a step forward, shoved it directly into his gut.

"To what do I owe this pleasure?" he demanded, black eyes narrowing.

"Where's my sister? What did you do with Tansy?"

"Tansy." His grimace could almost pass for a smile. "Maybe you oughta be askin' what she did to me."

"Then you do have her!"

"Whoa! She *was* here."

Excitement seared Willow. "Where is she now?"

"If I knew, I'd wring her scrawny neck."

Furious at the threat to her sister, Willow again shoved the shotgun into his gut. Her mistake. Fast as lightning, Madrid grabbed the barrel and twisted in one smooth motion. Magically, the weapon was in his hand rather than in hers.

Willow froze. Now she'd gone and done it. Now he'd shoot her with her own shotgun. Rather, with Hazel's.

But all he said was, "You won't mind if I just hold on to this until you're ready to leave." He held the weapon with the barrel pointed at the floor.

"I'm not leaving until you tell me where to find my sister."

Sighing, he stepped back. "C'mon in. You look like you could use some coffee."

Willow hesitated. He didn't seem to be threatening her. Besides, she still had the canister of pepper gas. If forced, she would use it, and Madrid wouldn't know what hit him. He wouldn't be able to keep his eyes open, much less focus on her, for twenty minutes. If the accompanying literature was accurate, that was. She took a tentative step inside, vowing not to let down her guard.

A promise that was hard to keep when the man not only gave her coffee, but offered her some of his eggs scrambled with chorizo sausage and a fat piece of pan-toasted bread. Somehow, the fierce bounty hunter seemed less intimidating with a frying pan in his hand. She meant to refuse, but her growling stomach had other ideas. Rationalizing that she needed something to fortify her, Willow reluctantly accepted his offer. She took a few bites of the spicy mixture and washed down the food with a big slug of coffee that was strong enough to tan a cow's hide.

Swallowing, she said, "Back to Tansy. Why would you want to wring her neck?" A threat that she herself had often posed to her infuriating little sister.

Madrid stopped his fork halfway to his mouth. "She stole my horse. That's a hanging offense around these parts." Then he shoveled the eggs into his mouth.

"Why doesn't that surprise me?" Willow commented dryly. "Hanging seems to be a common solution to problems around here."

"Ah, now it's coming to me." His expression shifted, softened, what could pass for a smile kissing his otherwise grim mouth. "You're the dangerous lady who stopped those vigilantes from stringing up the gambler."

"That was me."

"Are all the women in your family like you and your sister?"

Willow doubted he meant that as a compliment. "If Tansy stole your horse, it wasn't because she's dishonest, but because she's desperate."

"To get away from you?"

A flush stole up Willow's neck. "You could say her running away is my fault. Not that she didn't deserve my wrath. I probably could've handled the situation better, though. Talked some sense into her rather than using threats." She was babbling. And Madrid was grinning. The flush deepened. "I've been looking for her for nearly a week!" Her turn to narrow her gaze at him. "And to think all that time I was running around, putting myself in danger, you had her held hostage right here—"

He cut her short. "I gave her shelter for a few days, is all. Then, you'll remember I told you, she stole my horse. Maybe she went home."

Willow's heart lightened a bit at the possibility. The tracker had said some of the tracks disappeared around a rocky area. Maybe Tansy had figured out what brought her back to the past and had stolen Madrid's horse so she could return to the pueblo and get home.

"I've gotta go." She rose abruptly to her feet and held her hand out. "The shotgun, please." Which was parked against the wall behind him.

"How do I know you won't use it on me?"

"You have my word. Not unless you give me reason."

A dark eyebrow flashed up at her. "Maybe I oughta go with you."

"Forget it!"

"There's still a matter of my horse," he reminded her.

Willow knew Madrid was waiting for her agreement, but whether or not he got it, she was certain he would do as he pleased.

"All right. But hurry."

The bounty hunter stuffed one last forkful of food in his mouth and washed it down, draining his mug. Then he left the table, swinging the shotgun up into the cradle of his arm as he led the way outside. Willow didn't have the nerve to ask him for the weapon again.

But Madrid had barely mounted his horse before she took off, straight for Mesa Milagro. He followed, staying spitting distance behind her nearly all the way to the site. Suddenly he was next to her.

"I came across your sister just ahead—"

"I know. At the stream." When his forehead furrowed, she said, "I checked out the prints. Anyone could have seen two people rode away on one horse."

"Not just anyone."

Now that sounded like a compliment, Willow thought. "I'm no bounty hunter. I know my limitations." Thinking they both had a reason to want to find Tansy, she said, "You, on the other hand, could probably track down anyone."

"Anyone but a slippery jackrabbit like Barnabas Dunwoody," he grumbled.

Startled, Willow asked, "The Brother Bart's Tonic salesman?"

"More like a con man. He's wanted in towns from here to the Mississippi. Quite a price on his head."

It took all kinds, Willow thought, dismounting several yards from the stream and looking for fresh footprints. The set she checked out didn't belong to Tansy. Maybe her sister had decided to wait for water until she got home. Dunwoody, then? Hard to believe he was the criminal type. He'd been a pleasant little man, undoubtedly a precursor for salesman and con man alike.

"So how did Dunwoody get away from you?"

"He disappeared. I followed his tracks into the pueblo ruins," he said, pointing to the cliff dwelling. "They just stopped."

"At the kiva." When his eyes widened slightly, she knew she'd hit on the truth. Starting toward the ruins herself, she checked the ground, hoping against hope to find prints belonging to her sister. "Maybe Dunwoody learned its secret."

At her side, Madrid asked, "What in tarnation are you getting at?"

He'd probably think she was crazy, but what did she care? "If Tansy went home, that's how she did it. Through the kiva. The house you're living in belongs to Rancho Milagro, our spread, named after the mesa."

"No such ranch, and—"

"Not now. But there will be in the future. That's where we came from. The future. 1995. And maybe we're not the only ones who've traveled through time lately."

As she might have expected, Madrid howled with laughter. Willow moved faster up the incline, Tequila in tow, so that she would be prepared to go straight home if she thought Tansy had. She still saw no sign of her sister, but, remembering there were more difficult ways to get up the mesa to the ruins, she'd wait until she arrived at the kiva to be disappointed.

One way or another, however, it seemed Madrid would be disappointed about his horse.

Disappointment.

Willow couldn't forget her major disappointment in Ryder. His handsome face haunted her as it undoubtedly would for the rest of her life. The thought of spending a lifetime without him saddened her. Why was that? She'd never needed anyone but family before, no matter how faulted that family had been. Part of her thought it wasn't fair—her possibly leaving Ryder like this, without warning. Without saying goodbye. He had saved her life. Twice. Another part of her thought how unfair he'd been not to tell her who he really was.

At the top of the incline, Willow hesitated only a moment before going straight to the kiva. Whatever she found—or didn't find—she would keep her cool. No way would she break down in front of Wolf Madrid.

Behind her, he was still snorting. "So, you think you're from the future."

"1995," she repeated.

"You been drinking Brother Bart's Tonic?"

"I've never tried it, though he offered me some."

The laughter in Madrid's voice died. "When was that?"

They'd reached the area just outside the kiva. She stared down at the ground. Only one set of fresh prints. Dunwoody's. She looked all around but found no trace of her sister. Hope deflated like air leaking out of a balloon. Tansy hadn't tried to go home, after all.

Against a lump in her throat the size of a boulder, she answered. "Yesterday morning, as a matter of fact." So much had happened since, it felt like aeons ago. "I remember, because right after he left, I spotted Tansy's bracelet in the display case. That's how I figured you'd know where she was."

"I don't understand."

"I'm certain it was her bracelet," she continued, "because I'm the one who bought it for her. I can't believe she gave it away—though I guess she figured she owed you and was trying to pay you back."

"You think Tansy gave me her bracelet in payment for some shelter and grub?"

"Are you saying you took it from her?"

Madrid scowled. "I'm saying, last I saw the damn thing, it was still on her wrist."

No, that couldn't be right. "Titus Whitiker told me he'd traded it for supplies—to *you.*"

"Then Titus Whitiker lied."

Staring into Madrid's expression that had gone all mean again, Willow shifted uneasily. Had the shopkeeper lied? Or was it Wolf Madrid who was lying?

About the bracelet.

About the stolen horse.

About his only helping her sister out.

Who in blue blazes was she supposed to believe?

RYDER FUMED AND FIDGETED all day waiting ror Willow to return to Red Mesa. When he couldn't stand it anymore, he decided to walk off his anger around suppertime.

But what exactly got him so riled up?

That Willow'd gone hunting for her sister alone? More like she might find Tansy and disappear without so much as a goodbye. The thought of Willow vanishing into thin air devastated Ryder. Never to see her again. Unthinkable. But he'd known it had to happen sometime. Just not now. Not when he hadn't even had a chance to say goodbye.

He was on the opposite side of the plaza when he spotted them. Willow riding alongside Wolf Madrid.

Willow and Madrid—the woman he wanted to see more than anyone with the man he'd be happy never to see again. What the hell were they doing together? And why would Willow have gone alone to find Madrid, knowing how dangerous the bounty hunter could be?

Not that Willow looked the least afraid of the man.

Then they took a corner and disappeared, and Ryder was left staring at nothing. But he was feeling something. Too much to be comfortable.

Rage...jealousy...abandonment.

Love.

To his horror, Ryder couldn't deny it. He'd been suckered into a state of mind that was not favorable to his well-being, not at all, and there wasn't a damn thing he could do about it!

RYDER TURNED HIS poker face on her all night, every time she tried to catch his eye. Willow guessed she didn't blame him. She took orders and served drinks, her body on automatic, her brain puzzling out her situation.

A saloon girl dead. Someone trying to kill her. Her sister missing for real now.

And Ryder a gunfighter rather than a gambler.

Did the pieces fit together to make a whole?

Maybe Madrid would have some answers after his face-to-face with Titus Whitiker. He'd promised to have a talk with the shopkeeper while he was in town, promised to find out why Titus had lied about his trading Tansy's bracelet.

If Titus *had* lied, Willow reminded herself, her suspicions aroused about Madrid, too.

Was there anyone she could trust in this whole town?

Her gaze wandered to Ryder. Certainly not him. And, though she'd known Ryder for so short a time, he was the one person in the world Willow most wanted to trust. She fought to keep her emotions hidden and was glad a while later when Ryder folded his hand and left the saloon.

No matter. The thought of trust in general lay heavily on her weary mind when the saloon closed and Willow retired for the night. She'd grown up with so little reason to depend on anyone but herself. Her caution had been justified.

Bad enough she'd never been able to count on her mother. Now it seemed that Audrey Kane had lied to her daughters, as well. Or at least she hadn't told them the truth, which was the same thing. Grandpa Jonah had been there for her and Tansy physically, but emotionally was another story. No wonder she'd been content to live such an insular life.

Experience had taught her well. She hadn't been willing to put her fate in someone else's hands. And she'd been right not to, Willow assured herself. Despite her doubts about him, she'd grown to trust Ryder...and had been kicked in the teeth for her trouble.

Mooning over the fact, she pushed open her door and stepped inside before realizing it wasn't locked. Adrenaline rushed through her as warning signals went off. Starting to back out, she froze at a commanding, "Don't!"

Without rising from the rickety chair where he sat, Ryder lit the dresser lamp. The shabby room pooled with gold, making it appear almost pretty. The pulse in her throat countered the thought. An illusion, just like he had been. She stared at her fancy man, and for the first time saw the ruffled shirt and embroidered vest for what they were—camouflage. Only he couldn't disguise the angry set to his mouth or the coldness in his eyes.

"What are you doing here?" she demanded, wishing she hadn't heard that weak, plaintive note in her voice.

"Waiting for you. Like I did all day. I was wondering if you learned something...something you should share," he said.

"No."

"Then the interest must be personal."

She frowned. "Interest?"

"Madrid." The name curled off his lips contemptuously.

Making Willow realize he must have seen them together. "Afraid I was leading him to you?" she asked, hoping to put him on the defensive.

"Me?"

"Game time is up...Mr. McCreery."

A thick, stunned silence was followed by a simple, "How did you find out?"

"Not me. Ramona. But you already knew that."

"Ramona knew who I was?"

He sounded genuinely surprised. Relief shattered Willow's composure, and her legs gave way. Swaying, she steadied herself against her bed. If he really didn't know, then Ramona couldn't have been blackmailing him...and he hadn't killed the saloon girl to keep her quiet. But he had killed several men, Willow reminded herself, at least according to *McCreery and the Quick-draw Kid*. Though she wanted to trust him, she couldn't let him sweet-talk her into forgetting to ask him about it.

"What's going on, Willow?"

Going to the bottom drawer of the dresser, she pulled out the *rebozo* and took from its folds two items. First she handed him the Wanted flyer. His gaze narrowed and his jaw clenched, but he said nothing.

Not until she handed him the dime novel. "I read it last night."

"I was afraid of that. I told you those things were trash. I told you they could ruin a man's life. T. S. Kane. Some ancestor of yours?"

"That's what we figure." Knowing she had to ask, that she needed to have the whole truth about him, she swallowed hard. "Ryder, did you or did you not kill those men?"

Silence stretched between them. The longer it grew, the more certain she was that she didn't want to hear the answer. Then he rose and set the dime novel on her dresser, and she thought he might leave without giving her one.

To her surprise, he said instead, "If I'm going to tell you everything, I need something to fortify me. You wouldn't have a bottle of tequila stashed in here? Whiskey? Brandy?" When she shook her head at all three, he said, "Well, I do. C'mon."

Willow found herself complying. Locking her door—for all the protection that offered her—she followed Ryder down the hall to his room. She had to know the truth, whatever it was. Hopefully, he intended to give it to her. The whole unexpurgated story.

When he opened the door to his suite, an inviting glow shone from the cut-crystal lamp, and cozy warmth reached out to her from the fireplace. Willow eyed the burning logs, thinking she would never take any fire for granted again. The smell of burning wood assaulting her senses left her too antsy to sit. She paced around the sofa as Ryder went straight to the table holding the bottle of brandy.

His back to her, he poured. When he turned, he was holding two glasses, one of which he offered to her.

She shook her head. "I don't think—"

"Take it. You may need it to stomach my story."

Willow took the drink from him so she would have something to do with her hands. Ryder stood before the fire and drained half his glass. His tension was noticeable. Suddenly jittery, Willow took a sip of the brandy, and as warmth quickly spread along her nerve endings, she perched on the sofa.

"So tell me," she said.

Ryder clenched and unclenched his jaw. "I've gotta start back a ways. More'n a dozen years ago. I was a kid then, my sister Leslie not much older. She was beautiful...had a real passion for life. Unfortunately, she was also too trusting. Got mixed up with the wrong man."

Just as she had, Willow thought, taking another sip of brandy. "What was wrong with him?"

"Billy Jo Tate was a little too handy with a gun. Our parents tried to tell Leslie he was dangerous, but she wouldn't listen. Said she was going to marry him. They forbade her to see him again. Wouldn't let her go out alone, though I knew she snuck out some nights. She was too wild for her own good."

Willow's throat was tight. She had this awful foreboding. "Sounds a little like Tansy."

"One of the reasons I wanted to help you find her," Ryder admitted. "The day it happened, I was out with the horses in the pasture. I heard a lot of hoopla. Billy Jo came for my sister in broad daylight this time, brought a couple of friends to back him up. I was running to the house when Pa came out on the stoop with his shotgun. Ma tried to stop him...to pull him inside...but it was too late. Billy Jo and his friends were already shooting.''

Willow's heart missed a beat. "They shot your parents?''

"Killed them. I went crazy. I ran for the bastards, thinking I'd kill them all bare-handed. They started shooting at me, laughing, playing with me. Suddenly, Leslie was in the midst of it, screaming at Billy Jo to stop...she just got in the way...then she was on the ground, clothes soaked with her own blood. She was still alive, but the bastard who said he loved her just took off. Him and his coward friends. Left her to die in my arms.''

He drained his glass and went back to the bottle for more. For a moment, Willow could do nothing but sit in frozen silence, the image of Ryder grieving over his sister as her life slipped away as real in her mind as if she'd been there.

Eyes stinging, she murmured, "How horrible." And took another sip of brandy herself. "I take it the sheriff didn't catch them."

"They fled the county. Disappeared. No one cared enough to go after them—I didn't have the clout. So I vowed I'd do it if it took the rest of my life." Looking haunted, Ryder slid into the chair. "I couldn't run the ranch by myself even if I wanted to. Wranglers did what they could to keep the place going, while I spent my days learning to use a gun. Then I couldn't pay my help...couldn't pay my bills...I lost everything. So

I rode away from the land I'd lived on all my life, hired out to other ranchers and worked on my draw on my own time. After a few years, I got so I was pretty fast. And damn accurate.''

Willow knew what came next. "And then you went after the men who killed your family."

Ryder nodded. "One at a time. It took me years to catch up to all of them, each hiding in a different state. I didn't just murder them like they did my parents and sister, you understand. They were all fair fights. Face-to-face. They had a chance they didn't give the Mc-Creerys." He downed more of the brandy. "I saved Billy Jo for last. I thought his death would be especially satisfying, but nothing could bring my family back. And with each man I killed, I lost part of myself, until I didn't know who I was anymore."

With a certainty that came from the telling of his story, Willow said, "Because you had respect for life. You weren't a killer in your heart." Knowing there was more, she asked, "So what happened after Billy Jo?"

"Nothing for a long time. Then, a bit more'n a year ago, this kid who called himself Quick-draw Kavanaugh found me in Kansas City. He'd heard about my reputation and was trying to build one of his own."

"And he challenged you to a gunfight," Willow guessed.

Ryder nodded. "I told him to get lost, to go back to his parents and grow up before he put on a man's weapon. I was turning my back on him when he went for his gun. I saw his move from the corner of my eye. I swear pure instinct made me go for my gun and shoot. I didn't have time to think. And I sure as hell didn't mean to kill him. Not some wet-behind-the-ears, seventeen-year-old kid with the dime novel that gave him the idea in his pocket.''

Chilled, Willow said, "You didn't have a choice. It was self-defense. He would have killed you.''

"I shoulda let him. I looked down into that face and saw myself before my family was killed. That could have been me." Finishing his drink, he rose and moved to the fireplace where he stared down into the flames. "But it wasn't. He was dead and I was alive. Only I didn't feel alive anymore. I walked away from Kansas City and everything that reminded me of the past."

"Including your name.''

"I didn't want some other green kid trying to make his reputation off mine. As much as I didn't want to live, I didn't want to die, either. And one of 'em woulda been good enough to outdraw me. So I got as far away from those ugly memories as I could. But the past has a way of following a man. It's always here," he said, his fingers tapping the spot over his heart. "I knew it was only a matter of time before it caught up to me for real. That rope had my name on it, Willow. You never shoulda rescued me."

"But you didn't kill Ramona.''

"Wrong victim, maybe. Right punishment. Whoever's offering that reward for me knows that."

Ryder sounded tormented. Willow couldn't help herself. She rose and joined him near the fireplace. His guilt was palpable. He wouldn't look at her. She laid her cheek against the back of his shoulder, breathed in the masculine scent that so stirred her, and ran her hand down his arm.

"You didn't deserve to be strung up, Ryder. I can't pretend to understand how one man can take another's life, but I imagine you didn't see any other way. I can hardly hold your wanting some kind of justice against you. This isn't the twentieth century,'' she said, thinking of Sheriff Landry's lackadaisical attitude. "The justice system has a long way to go." And then some. Even in her time, it wasn't perfect.

Plainly moved by her impassioned declaration, Ryder turned and faced her at last. He gently cupped her cheek in his hand and stared at her in wonder. Golden red reflections flickered over his handsome face that looked more open—dare she say vulnerable?—than she'd ever seen it. And his eyes, those beautiful blue eyes that had glittered so coldly less than an hour ago, were filled with something that she didn't want to put a name to. Something that frightened her.

"If only I could live someplace where a man didn't need a gun to prove himself," Ryder said, his tone fervent. "Then maybe I could start over with a clean slate. I could go east of the Mississippi, but living in some big city like New York...I might as well be dead. Might as well just stay here and wait for fate to catch up to me."

"Don't say that!"

Willow wanted to tell Ryder that he didn't need a gun to prove himself in the twentieth century, but what would be the point? He would never agree to go with her.

"You'll be gone soon," he murmured, his face drawing closer, his expression infinitely sad.

"I'll miss you terribly." The words flew from her mouth before she could think.

"Truth?"

She ran her fingers over the tip of his moustache. "Truth."

"What about Madrid?" Jealousy crept into his tone.

"He's Tansy's hero, not mine," she assured him softly. "I threatened to shoot him if he wouldn't tell me where she was. As it happens, he's as anxious to find my little sister as I am. Seems she stole his spare horse. And—"

Willow never finished, never had the chance to tell Ryder about the bracelet. His mouth interrupted hers in the most disturbing way possible. And the most rewarding.

All her longing, all her hopes, went into that kiss. Her heart nearly burst with happiness, even though she knew it might be short-lived. His telling her about his past restored her trust and made her ashamed that she'd doubted him. She knew it wasn't possible, but she wished with all her heart that they could be together forever.

So when he tried to put her aside as he had before, she hung on tightly. "You don't get rid of me so easily tonight," she whispered. "I'm only thinking about you...and I've always wanted to sleep in a fancy four-poster bed."

"That can be arranged. Though I don't know how much sleep you'll get."

When Ryder swung her up into his arms and headed for the bedroom, Willow bit the inside of her lip to keep from giggling. She still hadn't gotten the hang of being swept off her feet like a heroine in a dime novel. But she was beginning to suspect she could get used to it.

The bedroom was dark and far cooler than the sitting room. The air felt good on her already heated skin. But when Ryder helped her remove her dress and undergarments, her flesh pebbled and she shivered, more in anticipation of what was to come than from chill. Then she balanced her bare bottom against the mattress while he pulled off her boots, touching plenty of naked leg in the process. Warmth flowed inside her in waves of delicious pleasure.

Ryder dragged down the covers and patted the mattress. Willow slid onto the sheet and, getting to her knees, she pulled him to her for another kiss. Their lips met in an explosion of emotion and need—a powerful need for more of him. Urgently, Willow opened his vest and started tearing at the buttons of his shirt.

"Wait a minute," he said. "Do you know how expensive this shirt . . . oh, hell, rip it off!"

They laughed together as Willow used a bit more care unbuttoning the garment. But she sobered when she slipped her hands beneath the fine cotton material and felt his warm flesh against her palms, briefly tasted the healing flesh of his neck.

Groaning, Ryder buried his head in the crook of her shoulder. His hands kneaded her bottom, scooping and holding her close. She slid her arms around his back, lightly scraping her nails across his flesh. Soon he was nipping at her neck, the tumultuous sensations he created in her inspiring Willow to work his shirt and vest totally free. The garments slid to the floor. A moment later, his trousers and undergarments followed.

"Damn boots!" he muttered.

His turn to sit on the mattress edge and work them off, while Willow had access to the rest of him. Behind him, she slid her arms around his waist and explored from his stomach to thighs.

With an explosive sound, Ryder was upon her, snaking across the bed, taking her with him. Breathless, Willow landed on her back, Ryder's body tenting her, his mouth on her breast, his hand working its way down her belly. She felt him hard and ready against her thigh, and her woman's center responded, giving his fingers a damp warmth of welcome.

While Ryder touched her in smooth, slow strokes, Willow's need spiraled higher and higher. As if he sensed she wanted more, he laced his fingers through hers, spread her arms up and out, then nudged her legs open with a knee. Unerringly, he found her, pressing until she was parted and offering him entrance. He explored her pathway, slowly and delicately so as not to hurt her, making her anxious and restless until they were well and truly joined.

Nibbling at her ear, he said, "I suppose people must make love differently in the next century."

He was moving in her. Slowly. Torturously.

The room began to spin, and Willow laughed breathlessly. "The toys may be different, but it certainly couldn't feel any better than this."

"You gotta tell me about those toys later."

There were lots of things she wanted to tell him about, starting with how much she loved him. How much she would miss him . . .

But all that could wait.

For now she chose to shut out everything—everything but Ryder and the loving they shared.

For Willow feared the end would come soon enough.

Chapter Twelve

About to leave Ryder's suite at dawn the next morning, her boots in hand so as not to awaken him, Willow tiptoed out of the bedroom and into the sitting room. She'd barely slept. He'd made love to her most of the night. Then, curled around his body, she'd dozed for a while, but gradually reality had assaulted her.

Quietly, she opened the door and peeked out into the hall to make certain no one else was about. She didn't want anyone giving her more *helpful* advice about Ryder. They'd all been wrong about him—Farley, Benita and Cal Atchley—she knew that in her heart. She'd even asked Ryder about his relationship with Ramona between bouts of lovemaking. Laughing at her because he thought she was jealous, Ryder had sworn that he'd been friendly with the saloon girl, nothing more. She believed him.

The hall was deserted, so she slipped out of Ryder's suite, closing the door behind her.

Willow knew she loved Ryder with all her heart, and she was certain he felt something more than lust for her. But what good would it do them? Filled with grief at her imminent loss, she chose to escape so she could compose herself and not have to explain her feelings.

A moment later, she was in her own room, stripping off the clothes she'd hastily donned. She was about to hang the dress and petticoats on a peg, when she spotted the folded paper on the floor just inside the door. She stood frozen, staring, as if mesmerized by a snake.

Now what?

Hanging up the garments, Willow hesitated before swooping down on the document, wondering what it could be. Perhaps someone wanted to give her another helpful warning. Irritated, she snatched up the piece of paper and unfolded it. One look and her eyes widened, for the missive was written in Tansy's hand. Her heart throbbed a beat too fast, and she shook inside as she read:

> Willow,
> I'm in big trouble this time, just like Zoe in "The Bounty Hunter and the Captivating Countess." You remember, the first dime novel I read—I told you all about it. I'll wait for you at the top of Mesa Milagro, above the ruins. Meet me there as soon as possible, and bring your friend Ryder Smith.
>
> Tansy

Willow read the note twice and digested the message. Tansy in trouble was no news. That she was alive and well—so far, at least—was. Filled with joy that they would be reunited at last, she knew that she had to get to Mesa Milagro as fast as possible, before Tansy did another disappearing act. Guilt struck Willow upon realizing she would already be with her sister if she'd only stayed in her own bed.

While putting on her riding clothes, she read the note a third time. It was just like Tansy to refer to some Wolf Madrid story. And she was supposed to remember it? Not having the faintest idea what happened to Zoe, she shrugged. Why did her sister have to be so cryptic?

What did it matter? They would be together again. Finally. And they could return to their own sane world. She got on her knees and pulled her saddlebags from under her bed. She'd just thrown them on the mattress and was straightening when the door opened behind her.

She whipped around. "Ryder!" He must have heard her leave his suite, for he was fully dressed, his hat pulled low on his forehead. Still, she could see his expression was closed, his gaze glued to her leather bags.

"Going somewhere?" he asked too quietly.

Her pulse skittered and she swallowed. "It's Tansy." She retrieved the note from the bed and handed it to him. "She wants us to meet her."

Ryder's expression didn't change as he read. Silence stretched between them for a moment, and she knew he realized what she meant to do.

"You're gonna leave for home when you find her."

Hearing the sadness in his voice, she swallowed hard. "You knew I meant to." Willow couldn't look Ryder in the eye. If she did, she might cry again, and this time she might never stop. "If you don't want to come, I'll understand."

He threw the note on the bed. "I was invited. I reckon I'll see this through."

Wondering for a moment why he had been invited—how did Tansy even know who he was?—Willow was relieved. "Thank you, Ryder, I—"

"No need to say anything."

"Yes, there is. I don't know what's going to happen . . . I may not have the chance later . . . so I want to tell you . . . that I love you."

He cursed under his breath and a lump stuck in Willow's throat until he said, "I don't know how I'm gonna get along without you."

Tired of going it alone, of being responsible for everything and everyone in her life, Willow only wished Ryder could share it all with her. Truthful with herself, she wanted Ryder as her life's partner.

She was a lovesick fool. They lived in different times and there wasn't a damn thing she could do about it.

The thought haunted her as they made their way to the livery. Stayed with her after they mounted their horses and rode out of town. Fate was having its way with her once again, Willow thought. So why did she always have to wish for what she couldn't have?

Like a father who was around when she needed him.

Or a mother who cared enough to do what was best for her own daughters.

Even a grandpa who more than tolerated the burden Mama had forced on him.

But this . . . this was the worst. She'd never felt such a sense of loss, and she and Ryder weren't even separated yet. But the split was imminent.

Life really wasn't fair. She'd accepted all the difficulties life had dealt her. Burdened with responsibility, Willow hadn't been looking for love. But love had found her anyway, she thought, staring at the too-stiff back on the horse before her. And all too soon, love would be gone, no more than a distant memory.

A *very* distant memory, she thought bitterly. One hundred and ten years' worth.

She ripped her focus from the impending loss and concentrated on the gain. On seeing Tansy. On the note she'd left.

The Bounty Hunter and the Captivating Countess. What was that all about?

Concentrating on Tansy's cryptic message, wondering why she wanted to meet on a mesa, Willow wasn't aware of anything going on around her until Ryder brought the palomino to a squealing stop and she nearly ran him down. Tequila danced around Gold Rush, making Willow fight to regain control of the gelding.

"What's going on?" she asked Ryder.

"Who the hell is that?" he demanded, eyes slit against the morning sun.

Making Willow aware of another horse bearing down on them fast. She squinted, but mount and rider were enveloped in a cloud of dust.

Her heart skipped a beat as she hopefully murmured, "Maybe it's Tansy."

CONSUMED WITH MISERY that Willow soon would be lost to him, Ryder had let down his guard. Now, eager to go, Gold Rush pranced under him as he kept the horse in check. He was waiting to see who was following them. Were they about to meet up with Willow's sister at last?

But when he was able to separate their pursuer from the surrounding dust cloud, Ryder knew they weren't that lucky. Too late to go for his gun. Wolf Madrid pounded down on them, rifle already drawn. His past had just caught up to his present.

Madrid pulled up mere yards away, the rifle aimed at Ryder's chest. "Don't try anything you'll regret," he warned.

His last reason to fight already slipping away from him—for if Willow found her sister, she would be on her way home that very day—Ryder said, "I won't."

Then Willow horned in, demanding, "What are you doing following us, Madrid? And what's with the rifle?" She looked around as if trying to spot some unseen danger.

Madrid didn't respond. He didn't take his dark gaze off Ryder. "Your gambler friend here knows. Don't you, McCreery? Oh, I'll need your gun."

Ryder carefully slid the Colt .45 from its holster and turned the weapon so it was useless. Madrid snatched the gun from his hand and stuck the barrel in his own belt. He'd known this was coming, Ryder thought, that it had only been a matter of time. The time had come too soon. He wished it hadn't come at all.

Still, he had to know. "How did you find out?"

"Got hold of a Wanted flyer with your pretty face big as life. Put two and two together about the name."

"It's not the law who's after me."

"What's the difference who pays the reward?"

"There's no time for this nonsense," Willow interrupted angrily. "What's wrong with you, Madrid? That kid forced Ryder into a shoot-out and lost, is all. You've got real criminals to track down, like that con man, Barnabas Dunwoody. And I've still got my sister to find. We're on our way to Mesa Milagro to meet Tansy now."

"Give her my best."

But Willow wouldn't let it go. "I thought you wanted your horse back."

"A man can buy more horses than he can ever ride for a thousand dollars."

"Willow spoke the truth about Kavanaugh's death," Ryder put in. "The kid forced me to shoot him."

"No one can force you to kill another man."

"You're right. I could have let him plug me in the back the way he meant to. He wanted to make his name off me, Madrid." The mean face staring back at him tightened and Ryder took a wild guess. "Maybe a man like you knows something about that kind of situation."

"And what if I do?"

"Then you know I had no choice. I was cleared by the law." A week ago, Ryder wouldn't have argued so fiercely. A week ago, he might have resigned himself to justice catching up to him, like it almost had when Atchley's boys tried stringing him up. A week ago, he hadn't known a woman like Willow Kane existed. "The flyer says to contact the Kansas City Pinkerton Office, not the Sheriff's Department."

"*Someone* put a price on your head," Madrid reminded him, "and I intend to collect."

"Even if that means turning me over to someone out for revenge? You got a conscience, Madrid? Do you believe in anything beyond the ground you walk on?"

"That's nothing to you."

"But it will be to you, if you turn me over to some bastard who wants me dead because of something I couldn't avoid."

Fidgety, Willow piped in. "So help me, Madrid, if you screw around and hold us up long enough so that I don't find my sister, I'll come gunning for you my-self!" she threatened.

The bounty hunter's lips curved into what could pass for a smile. "I'll take the chance."

She changed tactics. "You can't do this, Madrid. You just can't. I thought there was some 'code of the West' that real men in this century lived by. Well, I think you're a real man, and if you give it some thought, you'll know what you're doing is wrong."

Her fighting for him both pleased Ryder and made him sad. Pleased because it told him she cared. Sad because it wouldn't change the outcome.

"Let her go," Ryder pleaded with Madrid. "No price on her head."

"She can take off any time she wants." Madrid took his eyes from Ryder, if not his weapon. "I have no quarrel with you, Willow. Go find your sister. Take Tansy home, wherever that is."

"Go on," Ryder urged, forcing a gruff tone. "I've been taking care of myself since I was a kid. I don't need you to do it for me."

Willow started as if he'd hit her. Still, she appeared torn, Ryder would give her that much. But in the end, she did exactly as he would have predicted. Exactly as he wanted, Ryder assured himself. She backed Te-quila off.

Then, her eyes filled with tears, her expression dis-traught, she wheeled the Appaloosa around and rode off, straight for Mesa Milagro.

RYDER HADN'T MEANT the brush-off the way he'd made it sound. Willow knew that. But his words had cut her deeply. They hadn't driven her away, though. Concern for her sister had set her off on the trail once more. She was almost there, thank heavens. Mesa Milagro loomed ahead, and Willow looked to the flat top above the ruins, as if she'd see a small figure waiting for her.

No such luck.

Something beyond what Willow could explain told her that her sister hadn't been fooling about being in big trouble. Always the practical one, Willow had never given much thought to following her instincts before—that had been Tansy's specialty. But then, she'd never traveled through time before, either. Such a mind-blowing experience would be enough to change anyone. And, oh, how she had changed.

Inured with adventure for the past week, Willow didn't know if she could return to the same staid and *lonely* life she'd left. And she certainly couldn't leave this century without making sure Ryder was free. Once she had hold of her slippery little sister, she would then figure out a way to get the man she loved away from the bounty hunter before Madrid could turn Ryder in. She didn't know how, but she'd manage it.

With all her knowledge of Wolf Madrid tales, Tansy should be able to figure out an inventive way to help, Willow thought, finally finding something positive about her sister's obsession with the dime novels.

The Bounty Hunter and the Captivating Countess.

Tansy in the same kind of trouble as the heroine, Zoe.

The comparison nagged at her. If only her memory wasn't confined to practical things....

Why had her sister been so cryptic? Why couldn't Tansy just explain the problem? Willow wondered. No doubt her sister's sense of the theatrical demanded she play out the scenario for all the drama she could wring from it.

Arriving at the foot of the mesa, Willow pondered the best route to get to the top. No way for her to bring Tequila all the way up on this side. To take the horse, she would have to circle the mesa around to its north face, where a rough-cut path led to the top. That meant more riding. Definitely more time. And not having been there since arriving in the past, Willow wasn't even certain the path was passable.

And time was of the essence ... too much had been wasted already.

So Willow chose her only other option. She dismounted and led Tequila as far as the ruins. The gelding was agitated. A whinny came from low in his throat, and when Willow stroked his neck, his flesh quivered as if the horse could pick up her own anxiety.

"I'm going to leave you here, boy. Don't you worry, I'll be back for you."

She was trying to assure herself more than she was him, of course. Her stomach was doing somersaults as she sought out her path to the top. Footholds in the rock face would be her ladder.

Her anxiety increased. What if she slipped? Fell? She couldn't think that way, Willow told herself. She had to be positive. She could manage it. She would get to the top in one piece. For Tansy.

She had no choice.

Taking a shaky breath that telegraphed exactly how thrilled she was at the prospect, Willow approached the notches carved into the rock by a human hand. High above, about halfway to the top of the mesa,

another ledge would offer her a chance for a small
break. She'd concentrate on getting that far as her
initial goal, so that the climb wouldn't appear quite so
intimidating.

Right. Like she could really fool herself.

At the rock wall, Willow inserted her left foot into
a ragged gash, her right hand into another, this one as
high as she could reach. Taking a deep breath, she
stepped up, found the next notch with her right foot
and reached with her left hand. Another step, her belly
tight against the mesa's face, its angle so steep as to
threaten her equilibrium if she so much as dared to
look down.

So don't look down!

Willow stared straight ahead as she inched upward.
She became familiar with every crack and fissure, not
to mention every shading and variation of the rock's
glowing red visage. Beneath her hand, stones skittered loose and rained down on her head. She didn't
let the unexpected shower stop her.

Step . . . reach . . . step . . . reach.

Limbs caught in the rhythm, she didn't stop moving until she attained her halfway goal.

She moved onto the ledge to catch her breath, leaning with her back against rock to stop her world from
spinning out of control. The area was sizable, with
crevices in its floor filled with sandy earth, from which
grew an array of stunted, high-desert plants—juniper
and piñon and a few cholla cacti.

She was almost there. Almost to Tansy.

Or was she?

It suddenly occurred to Willow that she wasn't even
certain her sister was atop the mesa, no matter the
message. What was wrong with her? Why hadn't she

checked before taking that first step up from the ruins? Stomach knotting, moving away from her secure wall, she craned her neck, trying to see the top of the mesa.

"Tansy!" Waiting a moment, she called out louder. "Tansy, honey, are you there?"

When no answer came, her heart fell, and Willow was certain she was on a fool's errand. If Tansy had been hurt so bad she couldn't answer, she certainly couldn't get herself to the proposed meeting place. Hope shattered once more, and she wasn't certain she could stand it.

Still, she shouted, "Tansy!" again.

This time a thin wail, calling her name, answered, "Willow!" Faint, but definitely a voice she recognized.

Willow's knees grew weak and her heart skipped a beat. Her sister was really there. All the days of searching, hoping, being disappointed were over.

"Tansy, tell me you're all right!" she begged.

But no such assurance echoed back at her.

Dear Lord, what if Tansy really was hurt? How would she get her sister down? An answer she'd have to figure out later. No time to lose.

"I'm coming! I'll be right there!"

Energy renewed, a determined Willow ran to the wall and began climbing again, this time with more confidence.

Step ... reach ... step ... reach.

Her calves burned and her shoulders ached as she nearly flew up the almost vertical rock face. She didn't even hesitate until her foot contacted loose stone and slipped from its perch just as she was shifting her weight.

Heart pounding, Willow hung there, suspended from one hand. It couldn't end like this—with her falling, being unable to get to her sister. She didn't want to think about what might happen to her. Mouth dry, nerves alight, she sought a new purchase for her foot. When her toes slid back into the crevice, she rested her forehead against the rock, but only for a moment. Then she continued on.

Just before reaching the top, she gasped out, "I'm coming, Tansy, hang on," more to bolster herself for those last few crucial steps than anything.

Willow didn't expect an answer. And as she threw herself over the edge of the mesa's nearly flat table, landing on all fours, she didn't expect to see Tansy running toward her, wild hair practically standing on end, freckles practically popping from a too-white face.

"I told you about Zoe," the teenager sobbed out. "I told you! Why don't you ever listen to me?"

Thinking Tansy must be delirious from the shock of her ordeal, Willow forced herself to her feet and held out her arms. Her sister flew into her embrace, still sobbing. Tansy clung to her as if she'd never let go. Cradling her, Willow cupped her chin and lifted her head so that she could look into those green eyes that were spouting twin waterworks. No sign of concussion, nor of fever, thank goodness. The girl was undoubtedly just scared sick.

"Shush now, I'm here," Willow crooned soothingly, the lump in her throat nearly choking her with emotion. She couldn't break down and cry again, not now.

Tansy blinked and looked around wildly. "But you don't understand—"

"Yes, I do, honey. I do."

Willow tightened her arms around her foolish little sister and thanked God that they were reunited at last. She'd been so afraid . . . she'd make certain that nothing like this ever happened again.

"I'll take care of you," Willow assured her. "I've always taken care of you the best way I knew how, haven't I?"

Tansy merely sobbed harder and tried to pull away.

"Your devotion is what I was counting on," came another voice, this one also familiar. "I figured she was the leverage I needed. So let's get it right this time, shall we . . . Ramona."

Chapter Thirteen

Ryder still couldn't believe he might never see Willow again, a more awful prospect than what might happen to him after Madrid got him back to town. He couldn't let it go at that. Couldn't give up now, not even if Willow had abandoned him for her sister. How could he blame her? She loved Tansy more than anyone and feared for the girl, while she knew he could look out for himself. Most times, anyhow.

Trussed up like a calf ready to be branded, the rope holding him to his saddle ungiving, he was trying to figure out how the hell he could get away from the bounty hunter and go after Willow, when he spotted a cloud of dust ahead.

"Someone with a burr in his saddle," he muttered.

"Not comin' to save your hide, McCreery."

Ryder had to agree when he saw who was in such an all-fired hurry. Titus Whitiker. The shopkeeper would no doubt gloat over Ryder's quandary. Indeed, when the man pulled up before them, he seemed mesmerized that Ryder's hands were tied to his saddle horn, his ankles to the stirrup irons. And Madrid had charge of Gold Rush's reins.

"What in tarnation's going on?"

The bounty hunter answered tersely. "I'm bringing a man in, is all."

"Someone offer a reward for Ramona's murderer?"

"He's wanted for killing a kid named Pete Kavanaugh."

Muttering to himself, Titus shook his head. Then he said, "Can't bring him in for that one, Madrid. Not for Ramona, neither."

Ryder started. Titus Whitiker defending *him?*

"Move out of the way, Whitiker," Madrid growled, hand caressing the gun on his thigh.

"Not until you listen to what I got to say. It's important."

"All right. Talk fast."

To Ryder's amazement, Titus Whitiker told them a twisted tale. All the pieces of murder and mayhem suddenly fit together. And not just for him. The next thing he knew, Wolf Madrid pulled his knife and freed Ryder's bonds.

Then all three men turned tail for Mesa Milagro.

"I'M SORRY! I was forced to write that note, but I tried to warn you! I did!" Tansy cried. "You mustn't have understood my message!"

Another reference to *The Bounty Hunter and the Captivating Countess*. A vague recollection finally stirred in Willow. Her sister telling her about an adventurous countess held captive by a murderer so that he could lure Wolf Madrid to his death....

Now she remembered!

Swallowing hard, Willow pulled away from Tansy and placed herself between her sister and Ramona Cruz's murderer, who had a rifle trained on them.

"Funny. I was halfway convinced Titus was the one, that he'd gone crazy with grief when your boy died." The tintype on the shelf in the store's private nook was clear in Willow's mind—the prototype for the Mc-Creery-Quick-draw cover. "Pete Kavanaugh *was* your son, wasn't he?"

The woman who called herself Velma Whitiker stared at Willow, unblinking. She was dressed in men's clothing, including a sheepskin-lined jacket, as if it were the dead of winter. She always did seem to be cold, Willow thought, as if she had ice water in her veins.

"You shouldn't of stole that Wanted flyer from me and threatened to tell Ryder McCreery about it before I could see to his justice." Velma's gaze narrowed and her tone grew suspicious. "Where is he, anyhow? He's supposed to be here!"

"He's coming," Willow hedged.

She wished she were telling the truth, as her plans for rescuing her sister and then Ryder evaporated. Dear Lord, she might never see Ryder again. The thought made her sick inside. As did the rifle pointed at her.

Wanting to understand what she could only guess at, Willow said, "I know why you hate Ryder...you think he murdered Pete...but why me?"

"*Tch-tch-tch.* Blackmail's not nice," Velma scolded.

"Blackmail?"

"Not legal, neither. That's why I killed you." Velma suddenly seemed confused. "Or thought I did. I shoulda done it like the others. Knives are so messy. So much blood. Poison is much neater and more reliable."

So it was Velma who'd dropped over the edge rather than her husband. She'd killed Ramona and had placed Ryder's lucky chip in the saloon girl's hand.

"How did you get Ryder's poker chip?"

"One time when I came to the Red Mesa to get Titus, I slipped one from the pile."

So she'd planned on framing Ryder all along.

Velma's eyes glittered strangely, pupils dilated and with a blankness that came from something other than grief, convincing Willow that the woman's state of mind had been helped along by artificial means. Willow remembered the belladonna canister next to Pete's picture. A drug that could sedate and bring sleep, also known as "deadly nightshade," belladonna could be addicting and hallucinogenic, and it could be downright poisonous if taken in too big a dose.

How much had Velma taken?

More important, Willow asked, "Who else did you kill?"

"Criminals, of course. Some of them, like McCreery, don't even get put in jail. What kinda justice is that? And the ones that do, shouldn't get out."

Another snatch of memory came to Willow. Of Sheriff Landry saying how weird it was that his prisoner died after being patched up....

"Like Emilio Cruz?"

Willow saw she'd hit on the truth and wondered if Ramona had guessed, too, if the saloon girl had been searching through Velma's things to find proof that the woman had murdered her brother. Instead, Ramona had gotten her hands on the Wanted flyer. Obviously, Ramona'd had a bit of a bad streak in her if she'd blackmailed Velma.

"Your brother liked my stew in particular," Velma was saying.

"My brother," Willow echoed, realizing the woman must have fed the prisoner belladonna-laced food.

"She really thinks you're this Ramona," Tansy whispered behind her. "When I went into the general store and traded her my bracelet for some supplies, she told me Ramona had been looking for me. Then she described you. I went with her willingly, thinking you were using a fake name for some reason. She's been holding me prisoner for days."

Indeed, Velma had addressed her as Ramona, Willow thought. She'd also said they needed to get it right this time. Ryder had guessed that her slight resemblance to the dead woman, when added to her wearing Ramona's coin-lined garments, had been making someone nervous. Too bad he hadn't figured out who.

Even with a gun pointed at her, Willow couldn't help feeling sorry for the woman. Between her grief over the loss of her boy and the drugs she'd undoubtedly taken to make herself feel better, the shopkeeper wasn't in her right mind. Poor lost soul.

Willow pitied Velma—no matter that she had become a murderer in her unbalanced quest for justice. Now Velma believed she hadn't successfully killed Ramona...or maybe she'd convinced herself that she hadn't because it was preferable to a dead woman coming back to haunt her...yet another factor that could have adversely affected her state of mind.

That last thought gave Willow an idea. She looked around for shelter, but, as on the ledge, only a few stunted trees and bushes thrived. Two horses were tied to one of the bigger piñons. Certainly no place to hide from a bullet. So she had to do it, had to be convincing. Calmly, slowly, she inched toward Velma.

In the best hollow, soothing, *ghostly* voice she could muster, she said, "It's time you stop trying to see justice done, Velma. It's too big a burden for one person."

"You stay where you are."

"That gun doesn't scare me." Hell if it didn't. Willow's stomach was knotted, her pulse was racing and her mouth had gone dry. She only hoped Velma couldn't tell. "You already killed me with that knife. But I'm willing to forgive you."

"You really are dead?" Fear threaded Velma's voice. "But you're willing to forgive me?"

"If only you'll put down the rifle so you don't hurt anyone again."

Appearing confused, Velma protested, "You already said I can't hurt you none."

Willow was nearly close enough now. "But the girl is innocent," she said, hoping that Tansy was staying safely behind her. Muscles coiled, she was ready to spring. "She's not a criminal. What justice would there be if you hurt her? Then *you* would be the guilty one."

"No!" Velma protested, gaze shifting toward Tansy for a second.

Seeing her opportunity, Willow lunged for the rifle. The weapon discharged, the shot going wild, its explosion followed by a high-pitched scream.

"Tansy!" Willow yelled, glancing back as her sister crumpled to the ground.

Locked together, both women were thrown by the unexpected. Willow thought to run to Tansy, but who knew what Velma would do then? Pump them both full of bullets? Anguish fueling her, she tore at the rifle. But the older woman was far stronger than she appeared to be. They wrestled for the weapon, turning and twirling, spinning across the smooth top of the slanted mesa.

Though she couldn't pull the rifle free, Willow refused to let go, not even when they neared the treacherous precipice. She took a quick look down—a straight drop to the desert floor—and began to sweat inside.

Velma didn't seem to notice. She kept on, jerking and screaming at Willow, all the while cursing the already dead Ramona. They were circling the perimeter of the mesa, every so often getting a bit too close to what could be sudden death.

Her world spinning around her, Willow hung on for dear life, until suddenly Velma hooked a foot around her ankle and gave a sharp tug. A surprised Willow went down hard, the breath knocked out of her, her head hanging over the edge of the mesa.

"You're no ghost!" Velma yelled, trembling. "You thought you could fool me!"

Beneath the screech of the woman's voice, Willow sensed rather than heard another sound. A light vibration shook the earth. Hoofbeats? Had Ryder come to her rescue, after all? But was it too late? Only a few yards away, Velma was raising the rifle, aiming it straight at her.

"Get ready to die, Ramona. I'll make certain you can't come back to haunt me this time!"

A shot rang out and Willow rolled to the side, something hard slashing into her ribs. She would have assumed she'd been hit but for the *ping* chewing up the earth next to her. Then she remembered what she'd forgotten to remove from her vest. Desperate, Willow reached into the pocket while bounding to her feet.

"Wait!" she shouted, stopping Velma from pulling the trigger again. "Listen. A horse is coming." The truth. She heard the clack of metal horseshoe against rock, followed by a winded snort. "Ryder McCreery is coming like you wanted." She only prayed it was Ryder rather than Titus.

Velma looked away just long enough for Willow to unsnap the leather protector and aim the canister. Taking a deep breath and squeezing her eyes shut, she sprayed pepper gas straight at the other woman, then backed off.

"A-a-ah-h-h!" Velma screeched, dropping the rifle. Her eyes shut to mere slits and began watering profusely. "You've blinded me!"

"Only temporarily." Willow wanted to get at the rifle, but she didn't dare step into the area she'd gassed for a while, or she might be sightless, too. Besides, she had more than herself to consider. Sick about her sister being shot, she called, "Tansy, are you okay?"

She turned her back on Velma to see her sister lying very still on the mesa's floor.

Her mistake.

Undoubtedly following the sound of her voice, the demented woman rushed and tackled her, the force of her attack sending both of them hurtling toward the mesa's rim. Panicked when she landed on her side and rolled, her legs propelling into thin air, Willow scrabbled for some purchase before the rest of her flew over the precipice, as well. She hooked her fingers into craggy fissures breaking up the hard surface. Her lower body followed her legs and bounced against the

rock face, her left knee absorbing the shock and pain.
Stars lit inside her head and her stomach turned over.

A yard away, Velma crouched on hands and knees,
tears streaming from closed eyes. Her palms slapped
against the ground, and a wail of frustration escaped
her. Heartbreaking sobs followed, the sounds of a
mother who had lost everything, even her revenge.

Then the sound of horses prancing and whinnying
intruded on Willow's reeling world.

"Willow!" a man roared. "Hold on!"

Recognizing the voice, she thanked God he'd come
in time. "Ryder, I'm trying!"

Her fingers burned, but Willow held on for all she
was worth. Head flat against the ground, she dared
not lift it to look for him, lest she slide farther.

"McCreery's here?" Velma asked, sniffling away
her tears. "Where's my rifle?"

Willow watched her stumble to her feet and closer
to the precipice. "Velma, watch out or you'll fall to
your death!" she warned her.

"You can't trick me again, Ramona." Velma was
reaching out, both arms spread as she staggered. "I'm
gonna find my rifle and do what I shoulda done when
we first came to town—shoot the bastard who killed
my boy!"

"Velma, no!" Titus shouted amid a flurry of leather
slapping rock.

But Velma was already taking the irreversible step
that transported her right over the precipice. Her feet
danced on air, her mouth made a large O, and her wail
of terror as she plummeted sent a chill crawling right
up Willow's spine. Numb with the shock of seeing
someone fall to her death, Willow hardly realized

fierce hands had gripped her upper arms and were pulling her to safety.

A sob tore from her throat, and Willow cried, "Tansy...she's been shot," as Ryder gathered her close and held her as if he never meant to let her go.

"Madrid's seeing to her now," he murmured in her hair, then kissed her ear, her forehead, and her cheek in succession. "C'mon."

Even as Ryder guided Willow to her sister, she glanced back at Titus, who stood stiffly at the precipice, staring out blankly, as if in a trance. She pitied him, too, though she wondered how involved he'd been in his wife's quest for revenge. He couldn't have been totally innocent, since he was going by the name Whitiker rather than Kavanaugh. And she'd seen firsthand how much he'd hated Ryder.

Then her whole attention centered on Tansy as she limped over to where Madrid was tending to her. He'd ripped off Tansy's shirtsleeve and was now tying it around her mangled upper arm.

"To stop the bleeding," the bounty hunter said gruffly. "Just a flesh wound."

Despite his reassurance, Willow knew something was terribly wrong. She could see it in his face. "Then why is she lying so still?"

"She hit her head on a rock." Gently, Madrid cradled Tansy's head and moved it slightly, so Willow could see a darker red drenching the girl's hair.

"Dear God," Willow whispered, falling to her knees at her sister's side. "Tansy, honey, please wake up."

She hesitated to touch the girl, lest she make it worse. Head injuries could be dangerous. And there

was so much blood. What if she wasn't simply unconscious, but in a coma?

"She needs time," Madrid said, his expression
scarier than she'd ever seen it because it was so trou-
bled.

"She's had time," Willow whispered, taking her
sister's hand, trying to rub some life back into it. "She
should have come to by now. Unless . . ."

Madrid removed his black bandanna and wrapped
it tight around Tansy's head, making certain the pad-
ded part of the folded material covered the wounded
area.

Standing behind her, Ryder kneaded Willow's
shoulders. "We'll get her back to town and to a doctor."

"No, not here!" Willow cried.

Nineteenth-century medicine was primitive. If the
injury was serious, Tansy needed the best medical attention she could get. Willow told herself not to panic,
to keep her head. She could get Tansy proper medical
care. She thought of the pueblo, so close and yet so
far. No way could they get the unconscious girl down
the side of the mesa. They would have to take the long
way around.

Her stricken gaze meeting Ryder's, Willow said, "I
have to get Tansy home as soon as possible!"

He nodded and signaled to Madrid. The men moved
away toward the horses. Willow stayed at her sister's
side, feeling for her pulse—slightly thready, if not hard
to find—and talking to her.

"Wake up, Tansy, it's time to go home now. You're
safe. Velma's gone. And you did good, warning me
like that in your note. If I'd paid more attention to
you, I would've understood what you were trying to

tell me. It's my fault, but I promise I'll pay more attention from now on.''

If Tansy was in a coma, chances were that on some level she could hear, could be compelled to fight, to come back to the one person who loved her more than anything. If she could, Willow would reach inside her and pull her back.

"I'm right sorry about your sister."

Willow started. Her gaze flew to Titus. He stood no more than a yard away, shoulders rounded, expression that of a defeated man. If he was looking for forgiveness, Willow could give him no succor.

"You should have thought about the possible consequences to innocent people before getting mixed up in some horrible revenge plot."

He shook his head. "I didn't know what Velma was up to until it was too late."

"You expect me to believe that, when you go around calling yourself Whitiker?"

"Velma's family name. We took it when we came west to start over. At least I thought that's what we were doing. I went along with what Velma wanted because she was so...disturbed over our boy's death. Till recently, I had no idea she'd hired a Pinkerton to track down McCreery and then put a price on his head. Velma could never face up to the truth about Pete. He was always a wild one, and she was always making excuses for him," Titus said sadly. "I hated McCreery for killing my son, but I didn't believe it was murder."

"You wanted Ryder hung," Willow said, even as he and Madrid returned with the horses.

"That's when I thought he'd killed Ramona. Atchley put it in my mind, 'cause of that poker chip he found in her hand. And then Velma ranted and raved and had me half-convinced that McCreery was evil, and that I was wrong about how Pete died. I got all mixed-up. She told me she got the bracelet from Madrid, too." He rubbed a hand over his face. "I didn't know how sick my woman was until I realized she'd gotten hold of your sister, planned to use the girl to lure you and McCreery to your deaths."

"That's what he told me and Madrid when he rode out here to stop her," Ryder confirmed, scooping Tansy up into his arms. "The reason I'm a free man now."

Ryder handed Tansy up to Madrid, who was already mounted. Willow couldn't help but notice how gently the bounty hunter cradled her sister, as if he actually liked Tansy and cared what happened to her—no matter that he'd threatened to wring her scrawny neck if he caught up with her. Tears stung the backs of her eyelids. Tansy was a handful, but she was normally a lovable handful. And she'd been so besotted with the novelized Wolf Madrid, she'd probably done everything she could to impress the real one.

Titus made a doleful noise at the back of his throat, and his eyes were shiny. "I'm just sorry I didn't get here in time to stop Velma from doing the girl or you harm, but I think she musta put something in my tea to make me sleep so long."

"Belladonna," Willow suggested. Wondering if he'd been drugged all along, she mounted up. "Let's get going."

They backtracked the way the men had come up, down the rough-cut trail on the side of the mesa opposite the pueblo. Ryder led the way, while Titus took up the rear. The excursion had never seemed to take so long before, but she had never before been in a hurry to get to the next century.

When they hit the desert floor, Titus mumbled, "Gotta find Velma, bring her home to bury her proper."

"You're a good man," Ryder said. "I only wish I could bring back your son."

"Pete made his own destiny." With a last glance at Willow, Titus moved off, leading Velma's horse.

"Titus!" Having thought about it, Willow decided she believed his story. When he turned in his saddle to gaze back at her, she said, "Thank you for coming to our rescue. If you hadn't..."

Titus tipped his hat to her, then rode off, his back straight. Willow only hoped Velma's body wasn't too horrible. He'd suffered more than enough for any one person, and it was obvious that he'd loved his wife as well as his son, and now both were lost to him. She was glad to go on.

When they rounded the far end of the mesa, Willow drew her horse alongside Madrid's and gave the unconscious girl cradled against his broad chest a worried look.

"Any sign of her waking?" she asked him.

The bounty hunter shook his head. "But her heart seems strong enough. I'm betting on her making it."

Meeting his black gaze, Willow forced a smile. "And I'm betting you'll get your horse back."

Madrid merely grunted his response to her attempt at humor. Willow's smile faded and she fell silent.

A few moments later, Ryder glanced back at them. "Almost there." He pointed to the pueblo ruins that were even then coming into sight.

Willow nodded. "Good." If things went well, she'd get Tansy help soon. She couldn't think about being parted from Ryder.

Madrid spoke up. "So you really think that place has some kinda magic, that you can get home from there?"

Madrid had never believed her claim about coming from the future. He'd laughed at her—though he wasn't laughing now. He actually looked . . . intrigued by the idea.

"We have to," Willow said fervently. "There is no other way I know of." She took a big breath. "I can't explain how a miracle works. I just believe. Mesa Milagro," she murmured, staring at the glowing red rock for a moment before locking gazes with him. "But then, I never thought what happened there was more than a legend, before it opened a crack in time for me . . . so why should you?"

Madrid appeared thoughtful, but took refuge in his own company once more, leaving Willow thinking about her going home and never seeing Ryder again. She'd never showed him she loved him, and now it looked as if the opportunity had passed her by. She brooded over the fact until they approached the pathway to the ruins.

How could she leave him? A glance at Tansy gave her reason. Her sister was part of her world, her responsibility, her family. Ryder was the man she loved, but, born a century apart, they weren't meant to be together. She'd never forget her fancy man, though. And every time she saw a Robert Redford movie, she'd think of Ryder.

And her heart would shatter, over and over again.

Since the steep incline would be hard on the horses if they carried human burdens, they dismounted to walk up. Willow gritted her teeth against the pain in her knee. Having left his horse at the stream, Madrid carried Tansy. Oddly enough, Ryder didn't leave his palomino behind. Did he really mean to give her Gold Rush to carry Tansy back to the ranch house?

Willow kept looking for signs of her sister's recovery, but kept being disappointed. The girl's face remained stark white against the brightness of her hair. And her pulse continued its thready beat. Even so, Willow was happy and hopeful when they reached the kiva, where Tequila whinnied in greeting. She patted the Appaloosa's neck.

"Hey, boy, I found Tansy like I said I would. You'll have to carry both of us home, but I know you can do it." And as the bounty hunter gently placed his burden against a ragged brick wall, Willow said, "By the way, I don't know if she told you or not, but Tansy named her horse Madrid, after you. Dime novels spread your reputation around pretty far and wide."

A dark brow flashed up. "When Tansy wakes, you tell her I'm mighty flattered."

The smile that followed softened the rugged planes of the bounty hunter's face, making him look almost handsome. Willow started. She'd had a low opinion of the man when she'd met him. Now everything was turned around. He might live on the edge, making his living off other people's misery, but he seemed to be a man of principle...and he seemed to have a heart. She could understand why Tansy worshiped Wolf Madrid—Willow was certainly grateful to him, herself.

"Thank you for taking care of my sister."

"She doesn't weigh much."

"I didn't mean just now. Before she made you want to wring her scrawny neck, too."

A smile stretching the planes of his rugged face, he waved and marched off, leaving her and Ryder alone for their goodbyes. Willow's eyes filled, but she was determined she wouldn't cry this time. She wouldn't have her blubbering like a three-year-old be the last image Ryder had to remember her by.

Blinking rapidly, she admitted, "I wish I didn't have to go."

"Why? Afraid you'll be bored? You've learned to like adventure too much?"

"I've learned to like *you* too much." She'd learned to *love* him too much, but all she could bring herself to say was, "I'll miss you."

"You don't have to, you know. You don't have to go alone."

Willow gave Ryder a disbelieving look. "You mean you're willing to come with us?"

"I don't have anything keeping me here. Or is it that you don't want me to see you home?"

See her home. He just wanted to make certain they arrived safe.

"I do want that," she said. Even if they were together only for a few more hours, she would savor the time with him. She'd be able to say a proper goodbye. She'd like to beg Ryder to stay in her world, but that would be unfair of her. She would settle for what he was willing to give her. "Of course I want you to."

Willow threw her arms around Ryder's neck and kissed him, knocking off both of their hats in the process. One of his hands slipped to the small of her back, the other to her head. To Willow's joy, he held her close and kissed her as if they were the only two people in the world.

Not that they were.

Tansy.

Reality intruding, remembering the reason for her hurry, Willow broke the embrace. She glanced at her sister, for the first time wondering if she could really force a miracle and get them home. Tansy wasn't looking one whit better. She was so still it scared Willow.

"So, what now?" Ryder asked.

"We wait."

She sat, carefully coddling her knee. She touched her sister, silently urging Tansy to fight, fight harder than she ever had in her life. She pulled Ryder down on her other side. Of course they would get home, and she would find a way to show Ryder she loved him. He slipped an arm around her, and she leaned back against him, grateful that she didn't have to go through this alone. That Ryder chose to be her anchor when she needed him.

She could lean against him like this forever...

"So, how does it happen?" he whispered, nuzzling her ear with his mouth.

"We pray." Exhausted, she indulged herself in the intimate feeling, allowed her eyes to flutter closed. "Please take us home in time to get help for Tansy," she whispered, praying that the mesa would once more live up to its name. She squeezed her sister's flaccid hand tight. "And let Tansy be okay."

Memories flooded her. She concentrated on the good times between her and Tansy, until she allowed herself to drift...

. . . anxiety and obstacles lifting from her, as if unseen hands took the burden. Then an image floated through her mind. He wore a white man's clothes and an Indian's moccasins. The tracker! Expression serious, he lifted a hand in greeting, then turned away, leaving her with a comforting feeling that was strange and yet familiar, leaving her one with the universe. . . .

. . . awakening when the sun blazed in her eyes. The golden sphere hung low in the west, casting a crimson radiance over the land she knew so well.

Willow sat with a start, waking Ryder.

"What happened?" he asked.

She didn't need proof. She just knew. "It's Kansas, Toto, and there's no place like home."

Before he could comment on her strange response, Tansy groaned, shifted restlessly, and blinked open her eyes. "Willow?" she croaked, her voice weak. "I just had the weirdest dream ever."

Chapter Fourteen

"Tansy will be absolutely fine once that arm heals,"
Doc Huggins said when he came out of her room after finishing his examination. "The head wound
wasn't nearly as bad as it looked ... though it seems
Tansy does have short-term amnesia. That means she
can remember everything that happened to her before
she got lost, but nothing of the past week."

"Is the memory loss permanent?" Audrey Kane
asked.

The people she loved had come together in this time
of crisis, just as it should be, Willow thought, squeezing Ryder's hand. No one had questioned his presence. Yet. And Grandpa Jonah hadn't even been
giving Mama a hard time, as he usually did.

"Hard to tell about memory loss," Doc Huggins
was saying. "Could be permanent. And then she
might remember bits and pieces of what happened to
her."

Snatches, as if she were having a dream, Willow
mused. Knowing that Tansy could get addicted to such
high adventure, she figured it might be better if the
past week stayed in her sister's subconscious forever.
If she remembered meeting Wolf Madrid in the flesh,

who knew what the hero-worshiping teenager might do?

"I'll walk you out to the car, Doc," Grandpa offered.

After the two men left together, Mama said, "I'll see to Tansy."

"No, wait." Willow hated being out of Ryder's company at all, since she didn't know how long they had together. But there were things she had to know. "Come to the living room for a few minutes, Mama, please." Then to Ryder, she said, "Mama and I have some talking to do."

Understanding lit Ryder's expression as he escorted her, his hand resting on her hip as if it belonged there. "I'll be over by the near pasture."

"I won't be long," she promised.

Mama seemed nervous, and Willow could hardly blame her. Everyone now knew the sheriff's deputies had found Tansy's horse by the stream and had been bewildered not only by her disappearance, but by Willow's, as well. One of the men had tried following Willow's tracks, but had lost them near the kiva. Some people were still puzzling over that.

But not her mother, Willow was certain.

"I have a peculiar tale to tell, Mama." Limping along the length of the room, Willow watched the woman who was an older version of Tansy. "You won't believe where we went off to."

"Really."

"Or maybe you would. Maybe you're more intimately acquainted with the legend of Mesa Milagro than you've ever said."

Her mother stared at her openmouthed, then swallowed hard. "I'm not certain I know—"

"Sure you do, Mama." Willow never had been able to tolerate game playing. She hated lies and deceit and feared her whole life was based on the same. "How old were you when you discovered the secret of the kiva?"

Audrey Kane sank down into a chair. She was trembling, and her green eyes shone with gathering tears. "Seventeen."

Two years older than Tansy is now. That would do it, all right. "Is that when you met my father?"

"Oh, God!"

"You did." Even though she'd guessed before, Willow felt as if the breath had been knocked out of her. "So that's why I never met him."

"You met him. You were only two. I wanted him to see you just that one time."

Sorrow filled Willow. "I don't even remember. Who was he? What did he do? What kind of a man was he?"

"He was part of the clan—one of the Pueblos who prayed for a miracle when the Spaniards trapped them in the cliff dwelling. He traveled a century forward in time. But he was alone. The people of his clan were scattered. He didn't know to when."

When rather than where. An odd concept. No odder than time travel itself, Willow guessed. "Tell me about him."

"He was so serious, not like me, always getting myself into some kind of trouble. I was running away from your Grandpa, again. I wished myself as far away as I could get that time. Hawk found me and took care of me. He was so kind. So handsome. Dark, penetrating eyes. Black hair. He looked more like his father than his Pueblo mother, probably because he dressed in white man's clothes except for—"

"His moccasins," Willow finished for her.

Mother and daughter stared at each other. Willow's heart pounded wildly and she felt a bit woozy. She hadn't been prepared for this.

"He was a tracker, off and on, for the U.S. Army," Mama said.

A tracker. Willow's eyes stung. She'd met her own father and hadn't known him.

"He helped look for Tansy," Willow whispered.

She remembered thinking the man looked familiar. Now she knew why. All she had to do was stare at her reflection in a mirror to see a feminine version of his face. Then a realization hit her—she might not have known him, but he had known her, which was probably the reason he'd been so sad on leaving her.

Willow found her voice. "If you loved my father, why did you leave him?"

"He wouldn't let me stay. He thought I should go back to my own world where I would be safe. He said he didn't know what his world was anymore. He certainly didn't want to make another leap in time. I did as he said . . . had you. I couldn't stay away, though. I kept going back to see him when I couldn't stand the loneliness, until he made me promise to stay away."

"All those times you left me with Grandpa and disappeared," Willow said, finally understanding something about her mother. "Does Grandpa know?"

Mama sighed. "I tried telling him, but I'm not certain he believes . . ."

Grandpa Jonah was pretty pragmatic, as Willow knew firsthand. "Why did you leave us with Grandpa, Mama? I mean the last time. Permanently. Was it because of me? You couldn't stand my being around you as a constant reminder of what you couldn't have?''

"No!" Mama protested, green eyes wide. "Of course not. I just couldn't take care of you properly on my own. I never even finished high school. The kind of jobs I got didn't support a family. And I couldn't live with Papa again. He never approved of me. I couldn't please him."

"So you shoved us on him?"

"Weren't no shoving going on," came a gruff male voice from the doorway.

Willow turned to face him. "Grandpa." She hadn't heard him enter.

"I took you girls in 'cause I wanted to. Audrey wasn't stable. That's why I told her that if she left you with me, she couldn't have you and Tansy back. Not ever."

"But why?" While she'd thought of her grandpa as being a bit cold, she'd never imagined he was cruel. "Why would you demand such a thing?"

"Because I loved you and Tansy too much. I failed my Audrey, and I wanted another chance to do it right."

"And I wanted a chance for you girls," Mama assured Willow. "I've regretted not being closer to you over the years, but I've never regretted doing what was best for you."

Willow stared at the two of them in shock. Once again her world had turned around.

Hadn't she wished for a mother who cared enough to do what was best for her own daughters? Hadn't she wished that her grandpa could have done more than tolerate the burden Mama saddled him with?

Hadn't she wished she had a father around when she needed him?

As it turned out, she'd had the first two all along, and now even her third longing had been granted.

Stunned, she had to know one more thing. "Tansy. Did you meet her father—"

"At a rodeo in Albuquerque," her mother interrupted. "I was lonely, and Jeb sure knew how to sit a bronc. I never got over your father, Willow, and I never will. That's why I've never married."

Filled with emotion, Willow stood, pulled her mother up and hugged her, then tugged her grandpa into their circle. The three of them clung to each other, and Willow felt emotionally better than ever before.

Until she thought about Ryder.

Willow broke the connection and stepped back. "Listen, you two see to Tansy. I have to talk to Ryder."

"Don't let go of your man, Willow, honey," Audrey Kane said with the authority of a woman who'd done just that. "Not if you love him as much as I think you do."

"I may not have a choice."

"We all have choices," Grandpa Jonah said. "You've grown up taking care of things around here. It's time you took care of yourself. If you...uh, gotta go elsewhere . . . I'll understand."

He was giving her permission to leave, if that's what she wanted. Touched, Willow hugged him and Mama again and said, "I love you both more than you'll ever know," then raced out to find Ryder.

IN THE DIMNESS of twilight, that magical time between daylight and dark, Ryder stood staring out at the cattle, trying to believe that anything was possible. That he could have a second chance.

How he envied Willow her stable life. A home. Honest work. People who loved her.

Family.

He'd give anything, do anything, to have all those comforts himself again. But with Willow. Only with her.

Not that he was worthy of a woman of such principle. He'd existed the last year on money made with cards. For an entire decade, hatred and the need for revenge had fueled him. Certain that men in this century didn't go around meting out punishment on their own, he figured Willow would never be able to get past that. She'd never want a man with blood on his hands to father her children.

Ryder heard her running up on him. The knee made her clumsy. He turned around and watched her hobble up the rise. Her long hair was loose and fluttered around her shoulders like a silky cape. Her expression was soft, her eyes luminous. What a beautiful picture, one he would have to keep next to his heart for the rest of his life, however long that might be. For without Willow by his side, he might as well be dead. Part of him would be.

When she came to a flying stop right in front of him, so close that he could easily take her in his arms, Ryder said, "Things went good between you and your folks." He could see it in her smile.

"Much better than I expected. I had no idea . . . but we can talk about them later."

Later. Would there really be a later?

"I reckon I can wait till morning to leave."

That'd give him a while longer with her, though he doubted they could be together in the intimate sense, not with her family around. He'd give anything to be able to hold her in his arms and make love to her all night.

"Then you're set on it," Willow murmured, and Ryder realized her smile had fled that tempting mouth, leaving it quivering. "Going back, I mean."

"It makes sense."

If he could even manage it, Ryder thought. He'd ridden on her coattails to get here. He wasn't certain he had what it took to go back alone. Who would listen to *his* prayers?

"Yes, sense," she echoed.

He tried to be practical for her sake. "We were born a century apart."

"But fate brought us together." Her eyes were shining, giving her a wounded look, and she was trembling. "Why, if only to separate us again?"

"We needed something from each other." He ran his fingertips along her jawline. "You needed help finding your sister."

"And what did you need, Ryder?" she asked softly, a desperation in her words that he'd heard before, but only for Tansy.

Ryder considered that. Danger brought people together, brought out their emotions, but that didn't mean the feelings were lasting, merely an extension of the self-preservation instinct. When the dust settled, the stars he saw in her eyes now would undoubtedly be gone. He was honored that she cared even a little.

And he would protect her from herself. So while he wanted to say that he'd needed *her* to give him back his humanity, to make him whole again, and that he still needed someone to believe in him, he gave her only a part of the truth.

"Atchley's boys would have finished what they'd started if you hadn't come along."

"Oh."

That Willow seemed disappointed moved Ryder. He couldn't resist taking her in his arms and holding her. She felt so right pressed against his heart. He nuzzled her hair, inhaled the woman scent of her that he would never forget.

"I wish things were different, Willow. I wish I came from a gentler time when a man didn't have to prove himself with a gun. I wish I could have a second chance to make things right. But wishing doesn't make things so."

"Why can't they? I wished to be reunited with Tansy, no matter what I had to do, or where I had to go to find her. What happened to me was a miracle."

"That's because of who you are."

"I'm nothing special," she protested. "It's because I wanted it more than anything. Because I believed it could happen."

Ryder wanted to spend the rest of his life with Willow more than anything. He just didn't believe a miracle could happen to him. He started to push her away from him, but she clung to his shirtfront, fisting his ruffles, and took a big breath as if preparing herself for a fight.

"I love you, Ryder McCreery. Tell me you don't love me back," she demanded.

His heart pounded at her admission. "I can't."

"Then tell me you won't leave me."

"I can't do that, either." For her own good.

She sighed and shoved at his chest. "Go ahead, then, run away. Be a coward. But I'm giving you notice that I'll be right behind you. I'll track you down wherever you go. You think Wolf Madrid's tough? There won't be a time in this universe where you can hide from me. *I* believe in miracles, remember."

Ryder could hardly believe his ears. She loved him enough to come after him. Just as she had her sister. He knew she would be foolish enough to do it, unless he convinced her otherwise.

"The past is no place for you!"

"Nor for you!" she snapped back. "Not anymore. You said so yourself."

"You can't come with me."

"You can't stop me. My father stopped my mother from being with him, and she's been lonely and miserable all her life because he was trying to be noble. We were *all* miserable half the time. I won't repeat her mistake."

Ryder heard the truth in her words, felt himself swaying, wanting to give in. Still...

"You're deluding yourself—"

"I know what I want. I want a fancy man, who's prettier'n me, especially when he wears a ruffled shirt and an embroidered vest. I want a desperado, who knows what it's like to stay alive through cunning and toughness. I want someone who can get my goat by pressing all the right buttons, someone who can make day-to-day living an adventure. *I want you!*"

That did it. Ryder grabbed Willow by the upper arms, jerked her to him and kissed her the way he'd been wanting to for an eternity. Her lips were soft, her body softer when she melted into him. And yet he knew how determined she was inside. Determined and passionate. A man could lose his good sense around a woman like her... and he was, after all, a mere man.

Ryder caved in and said, "Marry me, Willow."

Her answering smile lit her eyes. "As soon as we get home."

Hoping the past was behind them both for good, he murmured, "We're already in Kansas, Toto," before kissing her again.

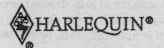 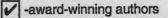

MILLION DOLLAR SWEEPSTAKES (III)

No purchase necessary. To enter, follow the directions published. Method of entry may vary. For eligibility, entries must be received no later than March 31, 1996. No liability is assumed for printing errors, lost, late or misdirected entries. Odds of winning are determined by the number of eligible entries distributed and received. Prizewinners will be determined no later than June 30, 1996.

Sweepstakes open to residents of the U.S. (except Puerto Rico), Canada, Europe and Taiwan who are 18 years of age or older. All applicable laws and regulations apply. Sweepstakes offer void wherever prohibited by law. Values of all prizes are in U.S. currency. This sweepstakes is presented by Torstar Corp., its subsidiaries and affiliates, in conjunction with book, merchandise and/or product offerings. For a copy of the Official Rules send a self-addressed, stamped envelope (WA residents need not affix return postage) to: MILLION DOLLAR SWEEPSTAKES (III) Rules, P.O. Box 4573, Blair, NE 68009, USA.

EXTRA BONUS PRIZE DRAWING

No purchase necessary. The Extra Bonus Prize will be awarded in a random drawing to be conducted no later than 5/30/96 from among all entries received. To qualify, entries must be received by 3/31/96 and comply with published directions. Drawing open to residents of the U.S. (except Puerto Rico), Canada, Europe and Taiwan who are 18 years of age or older. All applicable laws and regulations apply; offer void wherever prohibited by law. Odds of winning are dependent upon number of eligibile entries received. Prize is valued in U.S. currency. The offer is presented by Torstar Corp., its subsidiaries and affiliates in conjunction with book, merchandise and/or product offering. For a copy of the Official Rules governing this sweepstakes, send a self-addressed, stamped envelope (WA residents need not affix return postage) to: Extra Bonus Prize Drawing Rules, P.O. Box 4590, Blair, NE 68009, USA.

SWP-H1195

HARLEQUIN®

INTRIGUE®

L.A. Law, look out! Here comes…

Harlequin Intrigue is thrilled to continue M.J. Rodgers's exciting new miniseries, Justice Inc., featuring Seattle's legal sleuths. Follow this team of attorneys dedicated to defending the true spirit of the law—regardless of the dangers and desires in their way. Watch them take on extraordinary cases destined to become tomorrow's headlines…and to lead them to the love of a lifetime!

Don't miss a special Christmas Justice Inc.,
coming this December:

HEART VS. HUMBUG
Harlequin Intrigue #350

Available wherever Harlequin books are sold.

You're About to Become a *Privileged Woman*

Reap the rewards of fabulous free gifts and benefits with proofs-of-purchase from Harlequin and Silhouette books

Pages & Privileges™

It's our way of thanking you for buying our books at your favorite retail stores.

PROOF OF PURCHASE
HI-PP77
Offer expires October 31, 1996

Pages & Privileges ™

TM

**Harlequin and Silhouette—
the most privileged readers in the world!**

For more information about Harlequin and Silhouette's PAGES & PRIVILEGES program call the Pages & Privileges Benefits Desk: 1-503-794-2499

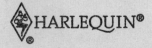

HARLEQUIN®

HI-PP77